THE FINAL BATH

by Amber Lenore Winckler

Text copyright © 2008 by Amber Lenore Winckler
Author photograph copyright © 2009
by Amber Lenore Winckler

Sassy Britches Publishing

www.amberwinckler.com

Bowker Books-in-Print
Winckler, Amber Lenore, 2009

ISBN 978-0-9842736-0-7

PREFACE

For as long as I can remember, I have been surrounded
by these blonde, beautiful smoking people.
Me— in all my blackness, finding myself time after time
sitting in the presence of my Mother or Martin (vital
people)
staring in awe at them—
All blonde and beautiful and smoking like demons from
Hell. Taking their long, lazy drags and then blowing
smoke out all around their words—
(around me.)
I get lost in the clouds.
I breathe them in deeply, knowing the dangers,
but unable to walk away.
You see, I have always believed
that everyone you really loved
killed you a little
just by breathing.

CHAPTER 1

I have seen thousands of dead bodies and I am not yet thirty years old.

I chose a career most people don't even want to think about, yet alone aspire to becoming. But wait, I get ahead of myself. Perhaps it is best if I start from the beginning...

Through the stained glass alcove shaped doorway of Atschuler-Stilson Mortuary there was a quiet peace. I arrived for my first day of duty in my best white sweater (the fluffy kind that made you want to reach out and touch it), and all the best intentions that only a recent graduate of mortuary college had the ignorance to possess. A list full of ideas consumed me before I even entered the back room. The building sighed with relief when I walked in; thankful hope had finally arrived... or was that just someone coughing? No matter. I was not bothered by mere trivialities. I was here to change the world.

The modest funeral home presented a large cream colored building with brown trim. This was not one of those fancy places with an attached cemetery and statues of naked Greek men on the lawn. Atschuler-Stilson Mortuary was a humble place with ancient but neatly trimmed Juniper bushes outside, a fair sized parking lot with an awning for the hearse to sit under during chapel services, and was conveniently located near the center of town (for all your death-care needs).

The caseload ran about 500 deaths a year. As one of the precious few family owned funeral homes in the area in these days of huge corporate takeovers, it was a testament to everything I believed funeral service should be... flexible, personal, caring.

The inner doors had ornate bronze hardware decorating them that had turned black with age and tears. The ceilings were high and the atmosphere slightly musty— but comfortable, like my grandma's house. It smelled of old moth balls and stale coffee, unassuming and average in every way.

I was introduced to Hank, the senior embalmer and arranger. He was a huge, hulking man with flaming red hair and ruddy, pitted skin. His eyes were watery and crystal blue; they made this strange ogre seem almost handsome, it seemed as if they belonged to a different face. Those sparkling eyes practically hissed within such a craggy mass of features. Hank made no effort to conceal his lack of confidence in me as he limply shook my hand with a wry smile. His rough working man's hands were lined with black oil that would never wash out of the cracks. They reminded me of my Dad's hands. My college instructors recommended that both men and women alike get regular manicures to ensure that they would present themselves professionally when meeting with families and doing paperwork. Hank did not appear to know this. Perhaps I would bring it up later when I felt more at home with him.

"Nice to meet you," he grumbled in a low voice, peeking at me under bushy red eyebrows.

"Nice to meet you," I replied.

"Louise has come to us straight from Cypress College," the manager, Aaron, informed Hank, who still failed to realize my choiceness.

Hank looked at me more suspiciously, "Have you ever worked in a mortuary before?"

I shook my head. "No."

Hank cracked a bemused half-smile and walked away shaking his head.

I raised my eyebrows and looked at Aaron. He patted me on the shoulder and said in his best funeral director voice, "Hank is a man of few words, my dear, but he is pleasant enough when you get to know him." He quickly turned and escorted me to the preparation room while continuing his reassuring tone. "These are the lockers. You can use the one on the end for your things. We only have three desks so we have to share with the other arrangers. It works out just fine unless we get very busy."

I looked in towards the desks and once Aaron saw my nod, he led me on through the hallway. We passed by caskets sitting on wheeled carts, white cabinets filled with urns and boxes, and a huge file cabinet with PRE-NEED written on a little card stuck in the front. The hall was actually quite cluttered and busy looking. Green wire stackable flower stands towered high and leaned in various directions, empty boxes and box cutters lay about as if someone had opened them in a hurry and then dashed away. A brown, rumpled man's suit jacket was slung over a cloth casket. Huge rolls of plastic were set up on steel posts. Thin gold colored boxes labeled 'crucifix' were neatly stacked high on the hallway shelves next to white candles in jars.

I pretended I was cool, hip, a woman of the world, ready for this moment that I had dreamed of for so long, but my stomach was doing flips and I felt a little sick. I tried to look at each thing and I had tons of questions, but Aaron kept his pace quick.

When we got to the end of the hallway Aaron brought our walk to a screeching halt in front of two big white double doors with a biohazard sticker on each and required warnings about which persons could enter. He turned to me dramatically.

"Do you know what room this is, Louise?" Aaron asked me with grave solemnity.

"The prep room," I answered quickly. Oh boy, I was good… fresh off my State Boards and a whole year of tests. There wasn't a question around that could catch me off-guard, by golly.

To my surprise, I saw Aaron's heavy brow furrow slightly. "Prep-ARATION room," he corrected me with a mildly stern tone. "We must always use the proper terminology. This is, after all, the most sacred room in the whole building. This is the room where we must always be observant and respectful. I must trust that all of my employees will uphold the honor and integrity of the bodies that our families entrust to us." He looked at me meaningfully, maybe even condescendingly, but I couldn't be sure; "Do you understand what I am telling you, Louise? Do you accept the burden of what we must do in this most sacred of places?"

I nodded dumbly, my quick college answers disappeared at once and I became a moron. Better just to nod. Aaron seemed pleased with my mute lameness. I silently cursed myself for not using the proper term for the room instead of the slang version.

"Welcome to the heart of our business." And with that, he opened both doors and held his arm out, indicating that I should go first.

Upon entering, I saw that the preparation room by far out-classed anything I had seen at Mortuary College. It was a huge amount of space with white cabinets lining the walls and twin stainless steel tables with hydraulic foot pedals on the ends. The tables gleamed bright silver, like they had just been shined. A white foam head with suture needles stuck into it at all angles sat on the counter blankly stared at us.

The embalming machines were on the white counter at the foot end of each table. The room was immaculate, particularly in contrast to the cluttered hallway, with nothing out of place and the pleasing aroma of lemon disinfectant.

I looked around for the familiar rusted out, blood spattered steel pushcarts with wheels that housed the instruments that seemed to exist in every preparation room that I had ever been in. There were none in sight.

"Where are the instrument carts?"

"That is a fine question. We keep our instruments in the cabinets because we feel that it is much cleaner that way." He opened the cabinet door for me so I could see the rows of cannulas, forceps, scissors, and all other types of embalming devices that were carefully arranged by way of size and shape on spotless white towels. "As you can see, we believe in the sanctity of keeping things as clean as possible. It honors God and the families we serve to do so."

The God talk really freaked me out, much as it had when Aaron turned it on at the interview, but such was my commitment and vigor for the job that nothing as trivial as a religious zealot was going to get in my way.

An embalmed body covered in a white sheet lay on a dressing table on the far side of the room. I walked over to inspect the work. It was an old woman. Her face had the white cream that embalmers apply after embalming so the tissues do not dehydrate. Her short grey hair was brushed back from her face. Her features were set in a pleasant expression, her mouth relaxed but closed, her eyelashes properly separated, and her hands lay gently across her stomach. I did however take note that the eye closure was at an improper half-way point instead of the standard two-thirds closure recommended in the embalming textbook.

I made sure that I pointed this small oversight out to Aaron.

He pursed his lips and closed his eyes for a couple seconds as if trying to compose his thoughts. "You know Louise," he told me in his polite but stern way, "As Embalmers, we must be very careful when we judge a fellow Embalmer's work. God is the only one who has that power. I know that I pray before each embalming for God to help and to guide me through it and to give me the talent to do that person justice so that his or her family may look upon them and find peace."

There he was, flinging that God word around again. I nodded as if I was in complete agreement. Better to just go along with it. Soon enough, I would be alone in here to work my magic and everything would be fine. I shifted uncomfortably in my new shoes. Already I could feel a blister forming on one of my heels and it was not yet mid-morning. For some reason I could feel my cheeks getting hot.

I wanted to tell him a million ways that I understood what he was saying about the family finding peace through our work in preparation of the body, and that I had thought that very thing a thousand times. How could I make him understand my passion? I would make him proud, he would see. But when I tried to make my mouth say something wonderful and deeply moving that would forever comfort his doubts about me and make him sigh with the recognition of a true peer and a person of great virtue, nothing came out.

He took the opportunity to continue on, still wearing that same concerned expression, "This mortuary in particular is very special. The owners are Christian and so we are held to a higher authority." I pretended to look at the body once again. Then his look softened, "Have you found Jesus yet?"

"I...I'm, uh... not sure. Maybe."

"It is hard to work in a place such as this and not have faith. God's will is at work and here is where we see it most clearly. It is hard to give the families you serve faith and hope if you have none for yourself."

"Well," I smiled, "Jesus wasn't listed as a requirement on the job application."

He didn't smile back at me. "Ours is a very special God-given duty. It is important to society and not everyone is cut out for it." Aaron went on, walking about in precise little steps with his hands clasped together in front of him. His face was deep in thought and he looked at me from behind his large glasses, "This profession can take everything from you that you let it take."

I turned from the body after he spoke. "How do you mean?"

"I mean that every year I work here I lose a little more. I mean that every family I meet with takes a little piece of me and now twenty years later I find that I hardly have anything left. I mean that you cannot get this close to pain and have it leave no mark. There is no amount of financial compensation that can make it up to you. It is the nature of the beast, I'm afraid.

"Families have no doubt what they come here for. They have a defined objective when entering this building. As Funeral Directors, we have to define our own reasons for coming here each day."

Unable to take his direct stare for very long, I lowered my eyes nervously. This was a silent signal of a small fissure in my feeble young bravado.

"Are you prepared to do God's duty?" Aaron asked me.

"Yes." My voice came out pathetically wimpy. I cursed myself as we left the prep-ARATION room and vowed from that moment forward to only answer Aaron's questions in a resounding and confident woman voice.

I had no idea what I was doing. Isn't that the beauty of youth though? Too young to realize that you have no business doing what you have no business doing. Age and loss causes the fear of failure and begin the first whispers of self-doubt. I was not at that stage of life just yet.

My biggest concern that day would be the ketchup stain on my new white sweater. I could have cried over that corn dog/ketchup fiasco. I still mourn that sweater. It went so nicely with my black hair. Aaron's words (like most of Aaron's prophetic counsels) would not have meaning for me until much, much later.

I found out later that the body I had critiqued the eye closure on had been embalmed by Aaron. It was probably not the smartest thing in the world to insult the work of the Embalmer that I was apprenticing under at my first day on the job. I would have much rather been born naturally elegant, long limbed, pointy nosed, and socially graceful, but I had abandoned that dream long ago.

I prayed to Aaron's God that night to not let me do anything else to piss Aaron off, but Aaron's God was an angry God— his perverse essence ran deep. Aaron's God liked to watch me squirm.

CHAPTER 2

I met Martin the next day at the employee entrance by the locking gate.

He more sauntered than walked. His lean silhouette approached me with the morning sun at his back and I saw he had his olive green suit jacket draped over his shoulder. His tall, thin body and large shoulders made his clothes wear exceptionally well, with clean, smooth lines without a single unsightly bulge or defect. He had fine hair colored like white corn with the slightest hint of a cowlick in the back that made me smile the tiniest bit. His mile-long legs caught up to me quickly and as he drew closer I noticed his face was lined with that of middle age.

A huge smile broke across his long face like we were old friends and he stepped aside so I could enter first. I realized that I hadn't opened a door for myself since I had arrived. I shuddered with the realization that my days as a retail sales clerk were finally and truly over. After my two year embalming apprenticeship was over, I would have the world at my feet. The time would literally fly by... not to mention that I was positive I would pick everything up right away and with hardly any practice.

"You sure are tall," I said without thinking as I walked past him. He smelled faintly like vanilla and cigarette smoke.

Big hands with long fingers moved gracefully up to his front shirt pocket and retrieved a cigarette from a half-full pack of Marlboros. He reminded me of a cowboy or someone equally as cool. He lit up and took a long, lazy drag before he answered.

"That's what they tell me. I may not be too stinking bright, but I sure am tall."

"Well that's got to be good for something," I suggested wryly.

"It's good for all sorts of things... getting stuff off of tall shelves, waxing the top of the hearse, you name it," he bantered easily. "You must be Louise. I'm Martin." He took another long drag that killed nearly half his cigarette as we walked towards the door that led inside the back entrance to the building.

We shook hands.

"The girl whose place you are taking left in a bad way. She worked here five years and then BOOM, they fired her."

"That's a great icebreaker," I fired off at him. "What else you got?"

He glanced sideways at me, "I've got a lovely bunch of coconuts."

"I see."

"Do you smoke?" he asked, tilting the smoldering stick in my general direction.

"No."

"Damn," he snapped his agile fingers disappointedly. "The girl whose place you are taking used to be my smoking buddy." He smiled just a bit.

"It sounds like you might have some unresolved issues about her departure," I said flatly. He laughed and that made me very pleased at my sarcasm.

Martin reached around me to open the door as we approached, which made me smile. I smelled that faint vanilla/cigarette aroma again. It wasn't entirely unpleasant. I caught the first glimpse of his steely blue eyes as he looked at me over his sunglasses.

His lean face grinned. He let out his breath and smoke billowed out of his cavernous mouth and filled the space between us. We were best friends by the end of the week.

CHAPTER 3

"Come on," Hank said, rolling a covered cot out to the van, "I'll take you with me on this removal."

"I was going to sit in on an arrangement with Martin," I answered. I felt torn. It had been a week and it was the first time Hank had showed any interest in me whatsoever.

Hank shook his head. "You can learn that anytime. Come with me to pick this guy up."

I thought for a moment and then started to slip my arm through my jacket. "Okay."

He didn't move. "You don't have to wear that jacket. It's ninety degrees outside."

I was relieved and lay the jacket over my arm.

"This will be a bad one."

"I have probably seen worse." *(What in the hell was I talking about?)*

"I'm sure you have," he said quietly, leading me down the hall and smirking. He knew I was a fraud.

I shrugged. I had been on one other removal, which is the term we used for going to pick a body up at the place of death. It was at the local hospital.

I remember it well. It was the second day I was at the mortuary. Aaron drove the van. He had insisted that I wear my jacket. I braved through the pain of my blistered heel as we walked down endless overly bright and sterile hallways and then stood quietly next to Aaron as he spoke in hushed tones to a nurse and completed some paperwork. He looked over at me every so often to make sure that I was paying attention.

"You remember this for next time, because you may be alone," Aaron counseled me when the nurse went to make a copy of a form for us. *"And always be respectful to the nurses. And don't put your hands in your pockets, it looks unprofessional. Make sure to clasp your hands loosely in front of you."*

Aaron went on like that throughout the whole process.

"Don't ever let the body be uncovered."

"Make sure you have the right person. Always check the identification bracelet."

"Don't let the nurses rush you."

"When we get to the van, I want you to watch me load the cot. It can be a little tricky, especially if the person is heavy."

"If the family is present, always ask them if they would like to step out of the room while we place the decedent on the cot."

"Don't lean, Louise. Make sure you stand up straight and tall. People are watching you and judging

the mortuary based on what they see. Be proud to be a mortician."

Aaron was relentless in his pursuit of proper enunciation, terminology, and tactical execution of fine funeral service.

Hank's training tactics were less vocal. And now I was here with him, on that sweltering summer day, about to go and pick up our body. I was sure that after this, I would probably be able to go by myself from then on. After all, I had been one of the top students in my graduating class.

It took me a long time to get comfortable going anywhere with Hank. He wasn't smooth or controlled like Aaron. He always looked a little rumpled and tired, even in his best suit. Hank didn't try to control things too much, and for the most part, he stayed out of the family's way.

And his hands... cracked deep and black between the ridges— like he had been working on a car. In spite of what they taught us in school, I have to admit there was something rather comforting about a man who you knew went home at night and fiddled around with his car in the garage. It made him seem reachable... and honest.

I guess you could say that Hank was a somewhat handsome man, in a Tommy Lee Jones sort of way. He towered over everyone except Martin when he straightened to his full six feet, two inches (which he rarely did). Usually he just stood quietly hunched over with his shoulders rounded, looking bored, yet charmingly uneasy about being in a suit and tie.

I was excited because I had been listening to the other guys talk about how Hank was the king of the in-home removal. No matter how gracefully executed, the removal of a body was still inherently a mechanical process. Experience cut down on the margin of error, so to learn from someone like Hank was a huge honor.

Convalescent homes and hospitals like the one Aaron had taken me on had optimal removal conditions. Doorways and halls were built wide; buildings were equipped with ramps and entrances that were designed to facilitate efficient transport of people. Mechanized beds could be lowered or raised, side rails could be removed, and for the most part, the family was gone by the time we arrived. These types of removals could easily be done by one person.

We always sent a minimum of two people for in-home removals. In addition to looking more professional, it usually required two people to successfully negotiate a person's home. We often had to climb stairs, move furniture, or carry the body on a flexible body stretcher because the cot could not fit around an angled doorway or hall. Mobile homes were especially difficult and presented many unique issues in regards to space and construction.

When the family of a decedent chose to stay and watch the removal, we were nervous about things we could not control, like purge, or the releasing of the bowels. This could be upsetting for the family,.

Hank loaded the cot and I climbed into the passenger seat.

"What type of death is it?" I asked.

"A decomp."

'Decomp' was an abbreviation for a decomposed body.

Hank raised one of his eyebrows and added, "In a mobile home."

My heart started to beat a little faster. I tried to pretend like I was cool about it. No big deal.

Hank drove fast. He laughed like a little boy when we caught a tiny amount of air while speeding past a bump in the road. I found that I had a bit of stage fright as we drove. I had a million questions, but I was afraid to bug Hank too much, so I chewed on the inside of my lips as we sped along to the mobile home park, catching every possible elevation in the road so that Hank could catch some air in the van and then yell "EEEE-YESSSSS!" and slap the gray steering wheel with boyish glee. These were the only times I ever saw him look happy— abusing the company vehicles.

We turned into the Sunny Days Mobile Home Park and Hank stopped briefly at the large wooden kiosk and rolled down his window, letting a warm gush of hot air into our air-conditioned world.

"Yuck," I said, "It's so damn hot." I fanned myself with the paperwork.

The plexi-glass on the enclosure was scratched up with a dull yellow hue and a peeling map of the park was pinned up inside. He glanced quickly at the map, located the mobile home number that matched our paperwork and drove on through an endless maze that snaked deep into the community.

As we rounded the last curve toward the back, Hank veered the van towards the left and a strange smell hit me. I wrinkled my nose as he parked behind a police car in front of a modest looking single-wide with a small porch.

"Smell that?" Hank asked, smiling at me.

"Yes." I wrinkled my face.

He grabbed the paperwork from the visor, "That's our guy." He opened the door and jumped out.

I slowly climbed out of the passenger side. The smell was unmistakable now— it was the smell of decomposing human remains. It is an odor that will stay with me the rest of my life, sickeningly sweet and overpowering—recognizable in an instant. My eyes immediately started to water. I had been around dead bodies before, but none of them had smelled like this.

I looked at the banged up door to the man's house and then at the window and its lime green curtains with a little red cherry pattern. There were a bunch of newspapers strewn about in front of the door. It suddenly occurred to me that I didn't want to know what was inside there. I started to panic a little.

I walked around to the end of the van where Hank was. I was about to ask him to take me back and get someone else to do this, but I stopped myself. He already thought I was a joke, and if I chickened out now he would think I was completely worthless. I chewed a piece of my hair and waited nervously for instructions. I kept looking at those little red cherries on the curtains. I noticed flies on the window pane.

"Here, put these on." Hank handed me a mask and some gloves. "We don't normally wear gowns for removals, but this might get messy."

I shrugged my shoulders nonchalantly and geared up. My heart was pounding so hard I half expected Hank to ask me what that sound was. The heat was terrible. The mask and gown made it worse. My face was hot and sticky and it was hard to get my gloves on my sweaty hands.

A police officer came out the front door and waved to Hank. They spoke briefly and I saw the officer smiling and fanning his face with his paperwork. I waited by the van, not fully convinced yet that I could go into whatever nightmare awaited inside that mobile home.

A small flash caught my eye and I turned just in time to see a neighbor's small grey head peeking out her window at us. She ducked her head when she saw me look at her, and immediately pulled her frilly blue curtains closed.

I wiped my sweaty forehead. Maybe I would get lucky and just pass out. But if I passed out, Hank would know I was just a fraud. I braced myself and held onto the cot tightly.

Hank was waving at me to come up on the porch. I reluctantly obeyed, pushing the cot in front of me. The officer smiled and nodded my way as he passed to go down the steps. I just knew he was happy because he got to leave this horrible place.

The smell was definitely worse up on the porch.

"The cop said this guy had a lot of stuff, so we are going to make ourselves a pathway for the cot first. Just do what I do," Hank instructed.

"Ok." I stood close behind him.

When he opened the door, the wave of smell and heat hit me hard. I actually gagged. Immediately and without thinking, I started to back up instead of move forward.

Hank reached back and caught my wrist in his gloved hand, moving me forward with him. Without turning around he said, "Breathe through your mouth."

I noticed the corner of his eye crinkling, but I could not tell if he was actually laughing at me through his mask.

I opened my mouth and drew in a breath. It was much better, although the thought of the air in that home going into my lungs was something nightmares were made of.

The room was dim with all the curtains drawn. We made our way through stacks of old magazines, empty aquariums, papers, empty coffee cans, and everything else you can imagine. How anyone could live like that was beyond my scope of reality. I was going to mention it to Hank, but I thought better of it and held my tongue. I decided to just pretend like it was something I'd seen a hundred times. I would win his respect yet. He would see that I meant serious business when I took this job.

Hank reached down and started moving things to the side. I quickly did the same. Sweat beaded up on Hank's forehead. My eyes were wide and my mouth stayed open behind the mask. I accidentally took in air through my nose again and I gagged a little and then resisted the urge to cover my face and run screaming from the place. I silently chastised myself and took the next breath in through my mouth. I looked around for the body as I continued to clear a path.

"Where is he?" I asked.

"Over there," Hank said, pointing to my left. Drips of sweat now ran freely down his bright red face.

The dead man lay on a couch with heavily textured dark plaid fabric, swollen to the point of appearing ready to burst. The gases released in his body from the decomposing process had caused his tongue to protrude so that it was forced past his ripe, shiny lips, turning his face into a grisly expression of mock silliness. He was almost entirely marbled black and green from the forces that worked to return his body to dust. The skin on his scrotum was pulled tight and I stared in wonderment and horror at how huge and balloon-like it appeared in the dim light. He had a little blanket that was saturated in his body fluids over his legs and feet.

Ants were everywhere, moving over his body, falling into trails that lead across the floor and onto the carpet, causing me to unconsciously slap at my legs when I realized that we were probably getting ants on us as well. Maggots moved beneath his skin, occasionally popping out through an opening to wiggle in blind protest in the dim light. Moving closer, I also saw long black beetles and all sizes of flies.

My eyes followed one of the ant trails across the floor to the small kitchen, across the crooked linoleum squares, up the chipped cabinet that was missing a handle and onto the Scooby-Doo green countertop. The trail ended at a plate with two English Muffins sitting on it, toasted and ready to be enjoyed. A jar of grape jelly sat next to them, lid still on, along with a butter knife.

I just stared at the muffins. This man was going to eat his muffins with jelly and lay on his couch to watch some television. It was strange, the things that hit you. The smells were horrendous, the body and the bugs were shocking and unreal, these things are bad enough for sure.

But for me, it was those damned English Muffins; they were what made me face the fact that this guy was alive once.

"Hey!" Hank said sharply, noticing that I had not moved since spotting the body. "Let's do this and get out of here. Move it."

Hank had lowered the cot and moved it beside the couch. I tried not to think of all the things I was stepping on as I walked over to him.

"Grab his legs."

I grabbed his legs. The flesh felt soft and squishy and seemed to move beneath the small blanket. I winced and grabbed a hold of whatever I could.

Hank took the head end and said, "Now pull."

We pulled, but blobs of skin and hair came apart in Hank's gloves, while the body stayed put. I was able to move one foot about an inch before my own hands slid off. I felt the sweat running down my back.

The man had been there so long in the heat that his flesh had sort of melted into the couch. It was a big, gooey nightmare. I looked at Hank with wide eyes and waited for my next command.

"Take it all. Grab the cushions." Hank told me.

We just packed everything into the body bag— the man, the cushions, the bugs, the little blanket. There were maggots and ants moving everywhere, now that we had disturbed things. I could even hear them moving inside the body bag, wiggling around and smacking up in protest against the thick white plastic.

We raised the cot and led it to the door, carefully making our way past the three steps that led down from the porch. I ripped off my mask as soon as we stopped and took in a huge breath.

Hank loaded the cot and tore his gown off. His shirt was soaked with sweat on his back and around his armpits.

I reached to slam the rear door shut and Hank grabbed my hand.

"Never slam it on a removal." He gently pushed the door until I heard the lock latch itself. "Never."

"Why?" I asked.

He was wiping his face with a small towel. "Because, you just don't slam it closed after you pick up a body. It's rude."

"Okay."

He looked at me. "You did good."

"Thanks," I said softly, still lost in the experience and the thought that my makeup was probably running down my face by now. I walked slowly over to my side of the van.

We rode home with the windows down and Hank smoked a cigar. He told me it was a tradition to smoke when you had a stinky case in the van. The cigar smoke definitely took the edge off the odor.

As we pulled into the mortuary, Hank looked at me out of the corner of his eye and asked, "Did you see the English Muffins?"

"Yes," I said, surprised.

He looked down and smashed out his cigar in the ashtray. "Yeah, I saw 'em too." Hank then jumped out of the van before I had a chance to respond.

Martin was outside leaning against the trash bin, smoking. "Hey, dorkus!" He called brightly as I approached. "How did it go?"

When I was in Mortuary College, we learned anatomical sciences, pathology, chemistry, restorative arts, religious rituals, and psychology terms. These courses were designed by educators to produce fine funeral service workers, which would then be dispersed throughout the country to practice fine funeral service.

We drew imaginary linear guides on dead bodies. We studied long hours in groups and alone, in school and after school. I carried my flashcards with me wherever I went. We were broken into groups and taught to locate and dissect out arteries. The importance of topographical disinfection and cleaning out all orifices was drilled into us. We had to turn in a report that focused on Tissue Gas, its causes and cures. All the teachers knew us by name. They fed us the hard sciences that we would need to pass the state board for embalming. To know these things was the only way that any of us would make good on our dreams.

And so I went to school and carefully dissected the fasciae from arteries and studied flashcards and stared at my teachers and tried to absorb it all even when I was exhausted.

My anatomy teacher in particular had a wonderful way when it came to teaching. Little drops of saliva would fly from the corners of his mouth when he got passionate about a subject or tangent. One time while he was talking to me, a drop of saliva flew out and landed in my left eye, and I swear that I didn't even blink. (Now that was devotion.)

Now with all of this training, you would think I was prepared for anything, but I don't think I recall them teaching me anything about English Muffins and the fact that their mere presence creates a link between my world and the world of the dead. My frustration about this gross oversight proved most unsettling for me. If things continued in this manner, I thought I might have to think about writing a letter of dissatisfaction to the educational advisory board at Mortuary College. I was righteous in my indignation at this horrible omission.

I drove over to my Mom's condo after work.

Mom lit a cigarette and held it with natural elegance as her large sapphire ring sparkled. Her house always smelled like something delicious and spiced was in the oven and the perpetually open windows allowed the soft breeze to play with the sheer pale ivory curtains. The entire home was the picture of taste and class. Fine original oil paintings hung on the walls. The couch was ivory silk and stuffed with soft down and was spilling over with different shapes and sizes of throw pillows in perfectly coordinating shades of rust, cream, and tan. Faceted crystal decanters filled with caramel colored liquids sat on shelves beside the stereo. The thick carpet had fresh vacuum lines across it.

Not a single thing was out of place. No old magazines, no trash (and no maggots.)

I crashed onto the sofa beside her.

Mom blew smoke in my face and scratched my back. I half-listened to her as she talked about how her boyfriend had sent her flowers and promised her that he would leave his wife. I knew that he would soon be living with her again. I lay numbly in the smoke. I closed my eyes and breathed it in.

Life could do that if it wanted to— make you scared. Make you hurt. Make you want your Mommy. I guess most of us were in the same sort of predicament. We spend our lives busy in a profession, but kept one ear carefully cocked— listening... waiting... hoping... for another mind (another voice), who thought the same; who breathed the same desires— who noticed the muffins rather than the maggots. The agony of this casual life was almost unbearable.

CHAPTER 4

Aaron decided it was time for him to supervise me during the embalming of my first case. Since Martin had only started three months before I did and was also Aaron's apprentice, Aaron thought he could kill two birds with one stone by having us both assist at once.

We all began to suit up in our personal protective equipment. I found that I had regained my composure after my removal that I went on with Hank the day before. A good night's sleep and some hot tea had proved the ticket. Indeed, I was feeling my usual spunky self. After all, the embalming lab was where I had excelled in school, winning the praise of my teachers for my perfect sutures and top-notch mouth closures. *Finally,* I thought, *the boys at the old mortuary would be able to see what I could do.*

I fiddled with my gown tie behind my back.

"Can I help you with that, sis?" Martin asked me, tying his own gown easily behind his back with help, no doubt, from his yardstick sized arms.

"I can do it myself," I said stubbornly, not looking at him.

He had a little smile in the corner of his mouth, the one he had a lot when he was watching me, "It works better if you tie the gown before you put your gloves on, you ding-a-ling."

Aaron snorted a little laugh.

I furrowed my brow and spent the next couple minutes fiddling with the damn thing before I got it tied. It wasn't a Boy Scout knot, but it would do.

Martin and Aaron both watched in bemused silence until I was finished.

I shot Martin a look using my most evil eye— which pleased him to no end.

Aaron started with a ten minute lecture on the morality aspect of dealing with human remains and how God was watching us and blah, blah, blah... I was chomping at the bit to show my stuff and redeem myself for all the stupid things I had done over the past almost two weeks of constant corrections and warnings, don't-dos, and must-dos.

I found myself losing track of Aaron's monotonous teachings. I began to look at Martin, who was across the prep table from me. The body lay between us and Aaron stood authoritatively at the head end. I thought it was strange how young Martin looked for an almost forty year old. His blonde hair was cut short and immaculately groomed (but for the cowlick), and was almost perfectly golden, unlike my mom, who had some hues of red in hers. Even his eyebrows were blonde. Together with his clear, light blue eyes, they produced a man whose fair simplicity was exceedingly gentle to look at.

Martin was bent slightly over the body and under Aaron's watchful eyes and constant instruction; he was cleaning the eyes out and inserting a thin plastic device called an eye-cap, which would hold the eyelids' convex shape even after the eyeball eventually sank from dehydration.

When Martin finished, Aaron adjusted the eye closure to exactly the wrong half way point (again); seemed satisfied, and then turned to me.

"Would you like to do the mouth suture, Louise?" Aaron asked, and then added, "Have you ever done one before?"

A mouth closing procedure of some kind had to be performed on all embalmed bodies. It kept the mouth closed during and after embalming. The simplest way was by using a device called a needle injector, which injected tiny pins with wires connected to them into the boney gums above the teeth. To close the mouth, the wires were simply wound together. On bodies with dentures, the bones in the jaw had often deteriorated to such a point where the pins had nothing solid enough to secure into, and in those cases, a more secure mouth suture was usually opted for. The mouth suture that Aaron had chosen for our dearly departed on that day was the Mandibular Suture (or Full McKue), which involved threading string around the mandible and through the nasal septum, adjusting tautness until the desired closure was attained, and then hiding the knot in the nose or mouth.

I took the needle and thread that he offered. "Of course, I have done these in school at least four times. I am really good at these."

I looked at the needle. It looked smaller than the ones we used in class. And, come to think of it, the thread looked different, too. It was thick and kind of sticky feeling.

"Have you ever used waxed thread before?" Aaron asked. His thick glasses had a thin layer of fog at the bottom right above his mask and I had trouble seeing his small quick eyes.

"Umm..." I almost lied, but then I changed my mind, "No. But I'm sure it's fine." I hunched down and began my mouth suture.

I started to insert the needle below the chin. My hands were trembling and for some reason I couldn't make them stop. I took a deep breath. It was really quiet and I could feel them both watching me.

I began my insertion again.

"You may want to make your insertion point within the natural fold below the chin," Aaron said gently, "It will be easier to hide that way."

I reinserted the needle as suggested. My hands were shaking like leaves and for some reason I couldn't get the needle around his mandible. I pulled and pulled until the needle was slightly bent. My cheeks started to feel hot. I didn't remember it being this difficult in school.

Aaron cleared his throat and handed me a curved needle. "For the inside, I find that this needle is easier. You can switch back to the 'S' shaped needle for going around the outside of the bone. Or better yet, work with a different needle on each end and meet in the mouth."

Martin was listening intently and nodding.

They were quiet again while I tried to thread the small curved needle. My hands were jittering uncontrollably and I felt like turning around to thread it so nobody could watch. They didn't even feel like my hands. This was not how I wanted my first embalming experience to go. It was only a freaking mouth suture for Pete's sake. Trying to make my hands stop shaking only made me more nervous.

Just about the time I was wondering when somebody would just shoot me and put me out of my misery, Aaron cleared his throat again and stepped closer to me.

He gently placed his hand on mine. "Now that I have had time to think about it," Aaron said carefully, "I think it would be better if you and Martin watch me do this one, and then I'll let one of you do the next one. I think it is always easier to learn when you see someone else do it first." He stared at me knowingly from behind his foggy glasses.

I let him take the unthreaded needle from my hand.

My mind raced with instant regret. *I already know how to do it*, I chastised myself inwardly, *I've done perfect mouth closures at least four (or maybe even five) times! Imagine me, crumbling under performance pressure— oh, the humanity!*

I looked at Martin, but he was watching Aaron complete the suture quickly and easily. I wondered what he was thinking. Maybe he wasn't looking at me because he would break up into fits of laughter if he did.

I could just hear him now, *'Can't even thread a needle? What a complete reject!'* My eyes squinted angrily at his lowered profile, indignant that he might possibly be thinking something like that.

Aaron asked me if I would like to make the incision to raise the standard artery used during embalming: the right common carotid. Now, a funny thing about that was in school, we were broken in groups of five people to a body. One person raised the arteries on the left arm, one the right arm, one raised the arteries on the left leg, one the right leg, and the fifth person took the head end and raised the right and left common carotid arteries at each side of the neck. We had lab once a week, on Wednesday, and each week we were told to rotate in order to a different leg, arm, or neck. The problem was, every time it had been my turn at the neck, someone was sick or missing, and I got bumped back to the right arm.

Of course I could recite the linear and anatomical guides we were forced to learn in school all day long— verbatim. But when it came to actually finding the carotid, arguably the singularly most important artery and the starting point of ninety-five percent of all embalming, well... I had absolutely no clue on what to do. It was a difficult artery to find, deep and below the jugular vein, cradled within the many muscles of the neck. At school, a common joke amongst the students was to declare the dead body they were searching unsuccessfully for a carotid on, a certified anomaly— a human being with no carotids at all.

I am ashamed and embarrassed to say that I had actually made it all the way through mortuary school without ever finding and raising a carotid on my own.

The gaps in my stunning academic career rivaled the Grand Canyon.

I was sure that if Aaron found out he would know he made a mistake hiring me. I had raised all the other, close to the surface arteries, so I would make a good try at this one. Maybe I would be surprised and it would be a cinch.

I recited the linear guide in my head. The linear guide is *an imaginary line extending from the anterior lobe of the ear to the sternoclavicular articulation.*

"I would like you to show me where you are going to make the incision before you cut," Aaron said as I readied my scalpel.

The transverse incision is made along the superior margin of the medial one-third of clavicle.

I drew an imaginary line with the dull end of my blade. "Here?" I asked.

He nodded his head. "That's fine, Louise. Go ahead and make your incision."

Martin nodded in agreement. I relaxed a little. My hands weren't shaking as bad as they did when I tried the mouth closure.

I ran the sharp blade across my imaginary line. *Not bad,* I thought to myself as I looked at the clean cut. I picked up an aneurysm hook in each hand. An aneurysm hook was an instrument with a straight handle and a little curve on one end, so it could be inserted below the skin to separate fasciae from the artery and then hook around the artery so it could be lifted or 'raised' enough to be prepared for injection of fluids. I began to separate the layers of adipose (fat) and stringy fasciae until I reached the muscle. I stopped and looked at Aaron.

"Good, Louise," he said, motioning for me to continue. "Keep going and look for the window in the muscle, the place where it naturally separates... the artery and vein will be right below that."

I tried to identify the window in the muscle, but it all looked the same to me. I fiddled with my aneurysm hooks within the incision until it became clear to all three of us that I didn't have the slightest idea what I was doing. I saw Martin wrinkling his brow out of the corner of my eye. My nose itched beneath my mask and I rubbed it across my shoulder.

"Just be careful, be gentle," Aaron cautioned me softly, "the jugular vein is anterior to the carotid, and it is very fragile. Make sure not to pop it before you raise the artery or it will begin to drain blood and you will never be able to see what you are doing in there."

It was deeper than I thought. I wasn't sure exactly where my guide was anymore. I dug around as it became more challenging. *The artery is located along the posterior medial aspect of the lower third of the sternocleidomastoid muscle.* I could say it and spell it right on tests... why couldn't I find it?

"Watch out there sis," Martin said, craning his long neck into my space so he could watch me better, "you almost popped the vein."

I used one aneurysm hook to pull back muscle and tendons so I could see if I had made it to the artery yet. I prayed to Aaron's God to let me find it. "Which one is the vein?" I finally asked, sighing.

Aaron looked at me as if he was making sure I was serious. His eyes squinted suspiciously. "It's the dark one there that you just ran through with your aneurysm hook."

I looked back down in time to see dark, thick blood drain slowly out of the broken vein, fill the incision and flow over onto the table like cold syrup. I cast an angry look up at Aaron's God. *Thanks for nothing,* I thought.

The blood that flowed was not pushed out because the heart had stopped, but the jugular was a natural drainage point and on bodies with blood congestion they could drain for some time before you could see anything in the incision again. Experienced embalmers like Aaron could have still easily found the artery blindly in the submerged site, but Martin and I had to visualize it first.

I heard Martin cluck his tongue and make a sound like "…tsk, tsk."

Aaron turned his head to one side and I heard a loud crack. "Well," he said, trying to sound good-natured, "Who wants to have a try at raising the femoral artery?" He immediately handed the scalpel to Martin, "Martin?"

Martin looked at me pompously. "Step right up here and watch the pro."

I watched Martin make his incision, juggle a couple of instruments around like an old-west gunslinger and produce that femoral in less than a minute; all while humming a happy little tune. Oh how I hated him sometimes. Martin hadn't even been to school yet (he was serving his apprenticeship first) and he was already a better Embalmer than I was.

"The next step is to thoroughly wash the body," Aaron finally said after we finished setting the features.

Aha! Now here was something I was good at. I immediately brightened and smiled beneath my mask. Nobody, (and I do mean nobody) could wash a dead

body like Louise Hammond. I was a body-washing fool.
Things were definitely looking up.

Martin and I both grabbed a germicidal soap bottle
and began washing the side of the body we were on.
Aaron stepped back out of our way and stood with his
hands clasped in front of him in careful observation.

I scrubbed the hair thoroughly and carefully used the
pointy end of a metal fingernail file to clean the dirt from
under the fingernails. I scrubbed the neck and in
between the toes and took pains to clean that dead body
in a way that would make Aaron's God proud.

"Hand me the hose," Martin said, "I am done with
my side."

I was still rinsing the hair. "I'm not done with it yet."

His gaze wandered to the neck of my gown, which
felt strange and loose. "Your gown came untied," he
noticed, stifling a giggle.

I thought I heard Aaron make a sound like a laugh,
but when I turned his way, he was looking innocently at
the ceiling.

"You are taking forever," Martin said, his eyes
shining impishly.

"That's because this water is trickling out," I
answered in a slightly frustrated tone, holding the hose
up so he could see how slowly the water trickled out.

Martin wrinkled his brow, "That doesn't look right."
He came over to my side and began checking the faucet
handle, pulling it off and on. Then he checked the hose.
"Hey dufus," he said, tapping my foot with his boot,
"you are standing on the hose."

"Oh…"I said, immediately lifting my own boot.

There wasn't much said after that.

The water bolus that had formed like a huge balloon in the rubber hose instantly was released; a perfect arc of water splattered across the paper anatomy charts pinned up on the wall behind us and splashed directly across Aaron's face before the emptied hose fell to the table like a dead snake.

I stared in mute horror as Aaron quietly removed his wet glasses and began to wipe his eyes. Water beads sat atop his tightly packed grey hair that resembled the flat top end of a scrub brush and formed tiny rivulets that traveled down his face and neck. Behind him, the anatomy charts began to wrinkle and ink started to run.

Shocked and horrified, I turned to Martin for help, but he just put his head down. His entire body was trembling in silent laughter.

In the back of my mind, I thought how glad I was that it was Friday. I had the whole weekend to regroup and re-strategize. Next week would be better. This might even be funny one day— but not on this day.

Somehow, we finished the case that will go down in my memory as the case that took a hundred years. I walked out of the mortuary that day a little shorter than I had entered, maybe even a little slower. Things were definitely not going as I had pictured them. I felt strange and unsure. This wasn't like school. This wasn't like anything I had ever dealt with before, and nobody could help me but me; and at the moment, I was a bumbling idiot. I didn't like feeling so helpless. I didn't want to be the new guy anymore.

Aaron saw through me with frightening ease. I ravaged my psyche with the suspicion that he somehow knew everything. He knew somehow that I would never make it as a mortician. My stomach tightened and adrenaline released into my body without purpose.

If the world's trees grew black hair dye and red lipstick, I'd have probably been quite fulfilled, but Aaron blew these things away with one steely gray look, my master Embalmer, my little religious fanatic. For two years, he would sign his name to each body I prepared after carefully assessing my work and correcting my technique. He was moody, deep, mischievous— sometimes infused with vitriol flair (if you were quick enough to catch it). He didn't let me get away with a single trick, right down to the end. He made it his passion to crush my ego and free me from its chains.

This was my mentor.

He was always somewhere way ahead of me, lost somewhere in a deeper thought or a more worthwhile concern... *(my salvation, perhaps.)*

I could only imagine how deeply he must have cared— to be so unmerciful.

Anxiety ridden, I went to Martin later that afternoon. He was in the carport smoking a thin cigarette. "I don't think that Aaron likes me very much," I admitted.

Martin laughed my worries off. "Awwww... he probably just wants to do you."

I made a strangled face. "What?!" I could not picture Aaron in a sexual context. "You are a heathen!" I was totally offended and instantly uptight.

Martin patted my head gently, "Don't worry about it there, sis, he likes you just fine. We all started off not knowing what to do."

"I know what to do!" I snapped, ready to unroll my list of academic accomplishments for him.

"Sure you do," he said, smiling. He took a long drag and blew his smoke in my direction. "Sure you do."

I regarded him with narrow eyes, anger instantly making me ready to undertake the task of showing all those men that I could take on the challenge. I turned and marched into the back entrance of the mortuary and heard Martin laughing behind me as the door swung shut on his playful words.

"You sure are cute when you march away mad..." he sang.

❉ ❉ ❉

Five people lost their lives that night while I slept next to my cat, Harold. Harold was a girl, but her name suited her and she didn't complain. It was a restless sleep with much tossing and turning, and it was filled with strange smoky visions of Aaron's dripping glasses and Martin's sparkling eyes. In one part of my dream, I tripped and sent a casket crashing into the side of the hearse... and then Hank ran by and ordered me to move all the flowers into the viewing room in a hurry because the family was out in the lobby, only when I tried to move one of the floral arrangements, it broke apart in my hands... and then I felt something moving in my coat pocket and I reached in to find it overflowing with plump, wriggling maggots...

I was mercifully awakened early the next morning by the sound of my phone ringing.

It was Joel, our fussiest Director/Embalmer, asking if I wouldn't mind coming in to help them out. I had plans with my mom for breakfast, but since I was still (in spite of the obvious) trying to make a good impression, of course I said yes.

Joel Bossy (he insisted that you pronounce it Boo-say) was our resident drunk. I soon discovered that practically every good mortuary had at least one. He was just a biscuit under thirty, but he looked and acted like a little old man. He even fooled his short, pear-shaped body into hunching over and feeling anguished long before its time. I was actually shocked when I found out that he was only a few years older than me.

I liked him right away, drawn to his fussy ways, his cynical comments, and his deep commitment to funeral service. He was from back East somewhere— Pennsylvania, I think.

"West Coast and East Coast funeral homes only remotely resemble one another in the fact that they both dispose of dead human bodies," Joel told me one day soon after I had started work. "Beyond that, they are on different planets, with the East of course, being far superior."

Joel resented the fact that so many people in California opted for cremation. He found it an abhorring concept and a waste of time to even write up a cremation contract; no headstones to design, no limos and hearses, no uniformed motor escorts, no commission. He explained to me that California funeral directors were to blame for their own inability to make the public see the value in viewing a loved one, or in the embalming process as an art form. In short, he declared haughtily over his peanut butter sandwich as we sat in the lunchroom that day, *"West Coast funeral directors wouldn't know how to stage a funeral for a dead cat."*

Joel came complete with his own reasons for being bitter and cynical, but I found that to be part of his charm. He seemed so lonely and vulnerable. Our relationship was tricky (like all of his interactions), how we got along each day varied with his moods and his degree of hangover. Joel was a true artist, as temperamental as he was talented. I watched him spend an hour one time trying to get a man's lip wax and color to look just right; later on he secretly admitted to me that he drove back to the mortuary in the middle of the night to do the lips all over again until he was satisfied before he could get any sleep.

Joel grumbled at me for asking too many questions and berated me for always hanging around him in the preparation room, he complained about how my intrusions were a constant hindrance to him, but he never chased me away. He let me know in no uncertain terms how abominable it was that I was unable to spread a properly thin layer of wax on a dead person's lips to save my life, but then he would carefully and painstakingly guide my hand until I finally got it right. We often waxed the lips of decedents prior to cosmetizing to prevent dehydration. This process involved using the heat of your hand or a hairdryer to warm and mold the wax into a gooey gel, which was then applied with a thin, flat metal tool we called a spatula. We spent hours in class learning the proper rolling technique and shaping technique, and recreating the natural lines and texture of the lips after the wax was set. If the waxing was done properly, people would never know it was there, but this

was one of the artistic skills that took work to master.
The alcohol fumes on Joel's breath when we worked in
such close proximity were heavy and sour, but it was all
part of the experience.

"I am an Embalmer. This is what I was born to do.
I'm not one of these hacks who just fell into because
their Daddy owned a mortuary! I have been licensed for
eleven years," Joel declared to me on more than one
occasion. The tone of his voice always sounded slightly
frustrated when he addressed me, but I think he kind of
enjoyed the fact that I was intrigued with his skills. As
testy as he could be, not even an unwilling teacher could
resist the flattery of awe and breathless close attention.

I often wondered in these early days if Aaron and the
owner of the mortuary (whom I had yet to meet) were
aware of Joel's drinking. I supposed they had to be
aware of it if I was. Perhaps they figured his talent made
it worth looking the other way on a few personal flaws. I
didn't think too much about it. When you are young,
you just accept things and allow them to be. I'm not
saying that its right, it just *is*. I was more concerned
about how I was going to afford to smog my car that
month than I was about Joel's deep and unabated
addiction and depression.

I arrived to work that Saturday and the mortuary was
alive with activity. Freshly washed cars and well dressed
people filled the parking lot. I straightened my gold
toned name tag over the ketchup stain on my fluffy white
sweater and walked into the back gate importantly. I was
sure that the people in the parking lot must have
recognized me as an important member of the staff right
away.

Joel was rushing out of the chapel with a floral arrangement under one arm and a leather register book under the other. "Oh thank God you're here," he said, grabbing my arm with his free hand and pulling me along with him. "Take these flowers to the cemetery and you can be my second man on this graveside. I need Martin to stay and meet with the new family."

He shoved the flowers into my arms and waved me off.

"Where is Martin?!" Joel raged to no one in particular as he stormed down the hall.

I loaded the flowers into the van and walked inside to grab the keys.

Martin glided into the room wearing a big grin, "Hey Lou, everyone's dying!" he exclaimed brightly.

I smiled to see him, "Where have you been? Joel's looking for you."

He loosened his tie, "Darlin', I've been busier than a one-legged man in an ass kicking contest."

We heard Joel coming quickly down the hallway and I dodged out the back door as I heard him begin to fire orders off at Martin.

By the time our graveside service had concluded, and I had witnessed the casket being lowered and buried (a service we offered for peace of mind since the family usually did not want to watch the actual interment) two more people died.

Back in the office, everyone scurried about. Only Hank looked nonchalant, looking over paperwork in front of his computer.

Joel flew by me in his pristine white lab coat on his way to the preparation room. "Did anyone see the

picture of Rosie Pratt that was on the counter?" He
called out as he disappeared into the room.

I shrugged my shoulders and kept walking.

Joel came grumbling back out of the preparation
room and slammed the door behind him. "I am going to
get this case ready as soon as I find her picture," he
growled at no one in particular. He looked over and
narrowed his gaze as he saw me. "Did you put the van
keys away yet?" He asked.

"No," I said, fishing around for them in my pocket, "I
was just about—"

"Good," Joel cut me off, "I need you to go to the
University to pick up a body."

Hank looked up from his papers. "I can go."

"No way are you leaving me here with all these
families to see," Joel snapped at him. He turned to me,
"Louise, you can do this by yourself... you are ready.
Just remember what I showed you about loading the cot
in the van, load head first, pull the lever just as you start
to go on, not too soon, and get some momentum going
first..." he grabbed a cot from its place near the wall and
steered it towards me. He eyed my sweater
disappointedly, "Is that a stain underneath your name
tag?"

I wheeled the cot out to the van. I could feel Hank
staring at me, concerned. He probably thought I couldn't
work the cot by myself, but he was in for a surprise
because I had been practicing taking the cot in and out of
the van all week.

I thought of how delicious it would be when I came
walking in nonchalantly an hour from now with the body
on my cot. They would think I was a natural. I became

joyful at the thought of it and I began to skip behind my cot on my way out to the van.

As it turned out, the University was really hard to find. My directions did not seem to correspond with actual streets. These were the days before GPS was standard on most vehicles. Back then, we had to rely on Thomas Brothers Guides. True, the Thomas Guide in the van was three years old, but come on, how fast could San Diego grow in just three short years?

I drove around for an hour. I could see the University in the valley below, I just couldn't seem to get to it. The roads in this damn city were all cork-screwed and littered with one-way streets. One minute I would be headed in the right direction, and the next minute I found myself headed back the other way.

Defeated and close to tears, I called the mortuary on the car phone to ask for help.

Hank answered.

I told him my problem and he was nice enough not to give me flack about it. He had me read street names until he could figure out where I was and then told me to stay on the line so he could guide me into the right parking lot.

"Turn in by the hospital emergency entrance," Hank said in his deep voice. "Do you see it yet?"

"No, not yet," I said, feeling a little more optimistic now that I was on the right track. I suddenly noticed the sign to my right. I brightened and screamed into the phone, "That's it! I see it! Thanks so much for—"

And then I slammed into the car in front of me. The phone was cradled between my shoulder and ear and hung there for a moment like time stopped before it fell to the floor.

I could hear Hank's deep voice sounding tiny inside the dropped receiver calling, "Louise! Louise! Are you there?!"

I reached for it blindly as I pulled the van off to the side of the road where the car I had rear-ended was parking. The man who exited the car ran to inspect his smashed fender before he looked up at me angrily.

I put the phone to my ear. Tears formed instantly in my eyes.

"Hank…" I began, but nothing came out. I felt myself sobbing with no sound. My nose began to run.

"You crashed didn't you?" He asked softly, more a statement than a question. He was so nice. Eighteen years of counseling grieving families really paid off in times like this. Unfortunately, his protectiveness just made me cry harder. I felt like such a fool.

I nodded into the phone, breaking into audible sobs.

"Are you okay?"

"I'm going to get fired, if that's what you mean," I blurted out pitifully. "I'm not hurt though."

"I'll come for you," he said.

"What about the body?"

"I'll call the removal service," Hank said matter-of-factly. "That's what we should have done in the first place. I'll be there in twenty minutes." He hung up.

I put my head down on the steering wheel and then the real tears came. I was convinced that my illustrious career in the funeral profession had flamed out as quickly as it had begun. Who was I kidding? I was not elegant and well-dressed like Martin or experienced and

authentic like Hank— word savvy and confident like
Aaron, or even obsessed with artistic detail like Joel. I
fumbled my clumsy way alongside them trying
desperately to take the good things they had to offer and
never sure which one I wanted to model myself after
more. If only I could find a way to smash all of them
together inside me and still end up a mortician that even
remotely resembled who I was. Was that possible?

I thought I had made a horrible mistake in thinking
that I could be a mortician. I was filled with social
flaws. I realized that I had spent all that time in school
but had learned nothing. I didn't even know where to
put the flowers at the graveside service I had been on
with Joel earlier (we had to move them all before we
could load the casket.)

What place did I have in a profession which valued
all the natural gifts that I did not possess?

When Hank finally drove up I flew into his big arms
without thinking. He hugged me tightly against his
barreled chest and said nothing. The van had been
loaded up on the tow truck and was being pulled slowly
away. The front fender was pushed down in the front
and the tow truck driver thought the tire might blow from
the friction it created.

"Come on," Hank said, taking me under his arm and
leading me to the company sedan, "I'll buy you a
burger."

"And a shake?" I asked, sniffling.

He scoffed like I should have known better than to
have to ask, "Of course."

"Could you just turn around and we'll head for the
Mexican border?" I asked Hank hopefully.

Hank smiled sideways at me and shook his head, "Gotta face the music, kid."

I was sure it would be my last meal and I was determined to enjoy it. I felt like the *Lady of Shallot* in the John William Waterhouse painting; going down the river with my head held high and clothed in my fluffy white sweater (the Lady of Shallot was also robed in white according to the Tennyson poem), my doom imminent and certain.

I shoved french fries into my mouth and wondered where I would be and what I would be doing six months from then. I reckoned that I would most certainly not be directing funerals. I ravaged that double cheese-burger on my final voyage to Camelot. By the time we arrived back at the mortuary, there was a thousand island stain next to the ketchup stain.

CHAPTER 5

Six months later I was still working at the mortuary. Aaron had never even mentioned the crash, with the exception of wanting to know if I was okay. In a few weeks, we had the van back with a shiny new front end and although Martin took the opportunity to call me 'crash' now and then, nobody else brought it up. I heard a rumor from Joel that the mysterious owner (whom I still had yet to meet) had a good belly laugh over the incident. Indeed, morticians were strange folk.

With good fortune (Aaron would call it God's Grace) on my side, I spent the months following the crash with a new attitude. I was an Embalmer's Apprentice who knew nothing, thought nothing. My only focus became to absorb the workings of the funeral home.

Each morning I came in early and emptied all the trashes. I picked the cigarettes out of the sandy pots outside the doors and rose up the flag on the pole out front. I kept a notebook of directions and carefully marked the way to and from places that I was sent on a regular basis; the crematory, the Health Department, the

Medical Examiner, the local hospitals, Universities, and convalescent homes.

As Apprentices, Martin and I were free to be bossed around by everyone who was licensed— and perhaps that was the biggest reason why we bonded tightly from the start. We formed an alliance out of insecurity and necessity over the many late nights we stayed to labor after the important people left the building.

We waxed the entire fleet one day, quite proud of ourselves until Hank came out and asked why we failed to wax the tops of the vans. We spent the next hour on ladders, waxing the van tops and communing over the injustice of our predicament.

A couple times a month Martin would mow the lawn and I would trim the ice-plant or suck up all the leaves in the parking lot with this huge beast of a motorized sucking push cart. We were always together— friends.

I discovered that school had not prepared me to deal with real life in a funeral home. My real education came from standing all day in the hot sun scrubbing rubber floor mats with comet, suiting up to climb into the body refrigerators to scrub them out with bleach, watching the way Aaron, Hank, and Joel handled making funeral arrangements and directing services— and all those late nights embalming with Martin, where we were forced to negotiate problem cases together before we could go to our empty homes and crash.

I had long traded in my fancy blister-causing shoes for soft black (flat) loafers. I found quickly that fancy shoes don't do a thing for someone who has to run a dozen floral pieces out to the van after a church service and then set them all up again at the cemetery— up hills, down hills, through wet grass, mud… (I did a lot of running around with flowers).

I also hung up my fluffy white sweater. My jobs were usually dirty or messy. I opted instead for dark suits to hide any evidence of my daily chores. My adorable patterned skirts were slowly being pushed further and further back in my closet as slacks now commanded the front. My necklines rose and my skirts lowered. It was a matter of necessity as I found that climbing in and out vans and maneuvering dead bodies out of tight places could cause some strange and unusual exhibitions of my womanly charms.

I am sure that I was single-handedly responsible for keeping Legg's Pantyhose in business that year. I had never seen so many pantyhose in my whole life. Sandal foot, sheer toe, control top, nude, beige, off-black, you name it— I had it. Nylons hung all over my bathroom, drying on every available surface after I had hand-washed them in the sink. Pantyhose swayed in the breeze caused by my ceiling fans. I had one huge drawer in my bureau solely dedicated to nylons. It made me feel uncomfortably like my Mom.

I traded in my fire engine red lipstick for gloss the color of pale plums. I removed my thumb ring and for the first time in my life, I bought (*and wore*) a wristwatch.

I can't really say when and why my conformity began— nobody forced me to change.

Some of my childhood friends said I had sold out; lost my identity.

Maybe…

But it didn't really matter— I was still the same girl in the end. My hands still got shaky when I was nervous, and I still chewed on my hair when I thought no one was looking, still ate too much, still said too many bad words, still looking for the best way to get rid of unwanted body hair, still young and hopeful, and still God-less.

Mom let her married boyfriend move back in. She said he was not drinking anymore and that everything was going to be fine between them...

I sat in on arrangements with anyone who wouldn't beat me away with a stick, and by the end of my first month I was permitted to make arrangements for simple services such as cremations and memorials. By the end of the second month, I was arranging Traditional Burial with Catholic Masses, and funerals with Full Military Honors at the local National Cemeteries.

I finally got the lip waxing thing down well enough so that Joel no longer felt compelled to re-cosmetize all my cases as soon as I left the room. Hank was a bit more skeptical and he never allowed me or Martin to embalm any of the bodies of the families that he had met with, although it was Hank in the end that very patiently and quietly stood behind me with his huge hands over mine and taught me how to find and raise the common carotid. Under Hank's firm grip, my hands were forced to finally learn the angles and secrets to making that elusive artery sit up and beg for me... success at last. Aaron could explain to me where that artery was for hours, to no avail. In the end, I needed Hank's big hands on mine. Hank's oil-stained hands contained the intuition and memory of raising the carotid thousands of times— and only when he guided me did it become truly clear. After that day with him, I never felt like I was digging around blindly again.

October passed, the month of my Birthday. Martin bought me a pair of fiery opal earrings (my birthstone), a surprisingly touching and personal gesture from someone with whom I bantered and competed with incessantly. He left them on my desk with a card and refused to acknowledge my profuse thank-yous, stopping only long enough to honk me squarely on the nose before dashing off with a file under one long, skinny arm.

It was a couple weeks until Christmas— the busy season. I was excited because number one; I loved Christmas, and number two; I was finally going to see the owner, who supposedly took the staff out to dinner the week before the Holiday. The great benefactor as yet still did not have a face. He remained a phantom. The only proof of his existence was a bunch of rumors and his signature at the bottom of my paycheck every two weeks.

CHAPTER 6

A teenage Hispanic boy died in a car crash the weekend before our employee Christmas party. He was coming back from a football game on one of the local rural roads when a dairy cow wandered into his path after having escaped its pasture by way of a undetected hole in the fence. The oblivious bovine did not even attempt to dodge the car and they met head-on, killing both driver and beast at the scene. Police determined the boy had been speeding and was most likely distracted.

The family scheduled the funeral on a Wednesday. We prepared for the service to be quite large; both because of the young man's age and the senseless and random nature of the accident.

I watched Hank work over several days to make the boy's body ready to view. Most of the cases we had at the mortuary were older in age, somewhat anticipated deaths, so a trauma case was a unique opportunity to learn the magic of the restorative arts. The boy's face had multiple abrasions, a torn right ear, and his skull was fractured into several large pieces.

Hank used wire to anchor the skull back together and filled the empty cranium with cotton and sealing powder. He cauterized the abrasions overnight with a strong phenol-based chemical. The next morning Hank came back in and filled in the broken skin with wax and used a hair dryer to shape it smooth and recreate facial lines and skin subtleties. He also sutured, cauterized and sealed the torn ear, using wax at the last to make the wound disappear before my very eyes.

The morning of the viewing Hank dressed the body and applied blended cosmetics over the boy's face using a long brush with coarse yellow bristles so that every defect vanished and I could no longer tell where there was wax. I watched and tried to memorize his consistent, little strokes, the way he held his brush, how he would add a dash of red or dark tan and then use the brush to blend, blend, blend, and the way he kept stepping back to check his progress. He used a huge soft black brush with a dark red handle to dust pressed rouge over the warm areas of the boy's face, cheekbones, forehead, nose, blending perfectly until the boy looked like he might simply have wandered into the mortuary and feel asleep on a stainless steel dressing table. I wondered if I would ever be able to do that...

Aaron ran the service and Martin and I were his helpers.

We arrived early that morning and cleaned up the chapel from the Rosary and Viewing the night before. Catholics traditionally held the service over two days; the first night holding a Rosary and Viewing usually at the mortuary. The second day a Mass was held at the Catholic Church, followed by a Graveside Committal service. I looked in the casket as I closed the lid and saw that all Hanks' carefully applied makeup had been smudged and the wax was smeared around and visible below (a common result of mourners who kissed and touched the deceased during the viewing).

We sealed the casket using a metal casket key that we inserted into the end and turned. We used a soft cloth to wipe all the fingerprints from the painted outer steel shell. We replaced the flower spray atop the casket and went to ready the vehicles next.

Martin and I washed the hearse and two vans. We shined up the wheels, chrome, and our shoes, loaded our flowers, casket, easels, prayer cards, boutonnières for the pallbearers, breath mints, and portable music system for the graveside. Then we both stood in front of the huge mirror in the hall by the preparation room and attended to our hair. We pushed and pulled at each other and told one another to beat it so we could each have the mirror to ourselves. That always was a good way to relieve stress before a big service.

"I look better than you," Martin purred with a sly smile, looking in the mirror while straightening his tie.

"No way," I retorted, putting on fresh lipstick. "You are old and ugly and I am young and beautiful…"

"And it's a damn good thing, too," he nodded, picking a piece of lint off the lapel of his warm camel colored suit. "Because you ain't that stinking bright."

"I'm brighter than your momma."

"My momma's dead," he replied, smirking.

I scowled, "Well, isn't that just so convenient for you?!"

Aaron came running down the hall and signaled us that it was time to leave. We walked out single-file, climbed into our shiny clean vehicles, and drove ceremoniously to the Church, confident in the knowledge that we were completely prepared for the events ahead of us on that day.

I sat up straight in my van, taking turns slowly so as not to disturb the vast amounts of floral pieces behind me. I still got that silly school-girl excitement in my tummy when I went on services. I liked to sit in the back and listen to the Pastors and family members talk. I would close my eyes as some of whom must have been the world's great undiscovered soloists belted out hymns that made me think that even Aaron's God must have cried when he heard. Martin always made it a point to look at me and wrinkle his large nose whenever we heard a soloist hit a bad note. He always tried to make me laugh during the service.

Martin and I loaded the flowers up after the Mass concluded and the pallbearers helped load the casket back into the hearse for its final journey to the cemetery. We drove our vans out immediately, leaving Aaron to drive the hearse leading the huge procession. The goal in funerals was to have the runners race to the cemetery and set up the flowers before the hearse arrived, so that the family never saw us hurrying, never saw anything but smooth, staged coordination. Our efforts were made so that nothing we did interfered with the family's experience.

We arrived at the cemetery and began hauling flowers out of the van and arranging them around the canopy that was set up for the family to sit under. We fussed for a few moments, making sure that an even amount of floral pieces would go on each side.

As Martin bent down to reposition an arrangement, his lighter and cigarettes fell out of his front shirt pocket, an event that happened several times a day, and one that always made us laugh and chime in together, "Wow... that never happened before," and then we would giggle like children. Funerals were always the most fun with Martin.

"Put the purple flowers over there," I directed him. "There needs to be a purple one on each side."

"But these two arrangements are meant to go together," Martin complained. He stepped back to get a better view.

I shook my head, "The colors are uneven, you dill-weed." I marched authoritatively over to the flowers, "See... yellow-yellow, purple-purple." I began cheekily shifting them around. "It should be yellow-purple, yellow-purple... and they should taper down in size, with the small pieces on the ends."

He tilted his head. "Okay," he conceded, "But it's not right."

"It is so right that you can't even handle it," I laughed. Then I turned thoughtfully, "You know, it is almost embarrassing— how much better I am than you. I think you should almost be embarrassed to stand next to me."

"I hate you," Martin retorted, smiling his biggest smile. He took out his cigarette pack and lit up, looking for a sign of the hearse. There was none. He checked his watch. "Aaron sure is taking a long time today."

I looked down the valley at the tiny road that was the only way into and out of the cemetery. "Maybe they stopped for lunch," I said, shrugging.

"That's not right. I'm hungry too," he feigned a whine.

"All I can say is, nobody coming into this cemetery had better have Little Caesar's on their breath," I said, shooting him my best disapproving look.

One of the young men from the cemetery crew came over to chat with us for a bit while we waited.

I looked down again and noticed one of the motor escorts just beginning to lead the hearse through the cemetery gates, followed by two limousines and a long procession of private vehicles. The cemetery worker waved goodbye to us and went back to his tractor. Martin tossed his butt to the ground and used one freshly shined black shoe to stomp it out. We assumed our positions beside the road, standing straight and tall, our hands clasped in front of us, looking utterly proper. *Of course, I looked better than Martin.*

Martin's job was to signal the hearse where to stop.

My job was to stop the family car at an acceptable distance behind the hearse (if they parked too close, we couldn't get the casket out), and then to make sure the long procession all had places to park. My next duty was to meet the family right outside the limo and lead them to their green folding chairs in front of the grave. My last duty as people left their cars to move towards the graveside was to make sure that everyone turned off their headlights. The motor escorts had cars turn their headlights on so they could tell if they were part of the procession in traffic, and as generally people are not used to using their headlights during the day, it was common for them to accidentally leave them on after they arrived at the cemetery and not be able to start their cars after the service concluded. Standard practice called for us to have jumper cables in all mortuary cars for such unfortunate events.

Martin and Aaron gathered the pallbearers and began instructing them using a great deal of hand gestures, as I made my rounds with the cars. I watched as six strong and able looking young men carried the casket and placed it on the metal device that would suspend it over the freshly dug grave, with a stoic Martin at the head end, and a somber looking Aaron at the foot end.

The huge crowd pressed in closer as more and more came from their cars. Aaron and Martin signaled the pallbearers to step to the side and made some minor adjustments to the casket before stepping to the side themselves. After waiting for the last attendees to arrive from their cars, Aaron bowed his head slightly to the Deacon, a signal that the service could begin.

The bald Deacon stepped majestically forward, his white robes swaying in the soft breeze, and began by sprinkling Holy Water on the casket and grave, a motion that started soft sobbing from the front rows. The Deacon addressed the crowd in Spanish and led them in a prayer that he read from a black leather book, his place held by a long ribbon of purple satin.

I looked around as the service continued in a language that I could not understand. It really was quite a large crowd. I wondered how we would control it if they all suddenly decided to rush the casket.

I could see the parents and other family members seated in the front row each reacting in their own, individual ways; some dabbing their eyes with tissue, some with their eyes closed and fists tight, some hugging, some sitting solemnly— showing nothing, refusing to break down in a public place. It was all grief.

I could hear the birds singing and see leaves drop intermittently off the huge Oak trees and float back and forth as they made their way to the ground. I looked at the back of Martin and Aaron's pressed suits— how professional they looked! I thought Martin might need a haircut soon, his cowlick looked suspiciously untamed (I vowed to tease him about it later.) Somewhere off in the distance I could hear a lawnmower humming, a sound that would usually send Hank flying down to the cemetery office to voice his opinion that it was rude to operate such equipment while a service was in progress. Hank and the lady who supervised the front office would then most likely engage in a shouting match that was far more disruptive to the service than any far-off lawnmower, standing in the doorway, him pointing a stubby, oil-cracked finger towards the noise and her shaking her blonde bee-hive passionately back in return.

It was a wonder to me how such things in this life just kept going around— like how I would probably go out to dinner with Martin after this and we would laugh and talk and debate the tactical execution of funeral we went on that day— what we did right and what we might improve upon for next time. And yet on that very same night, some other people would go home with one less family member above ground— walking by the closed door to his room and waiting in vain for him to come bounding out. Hugging relatives and hearing them try to give comfort, but unable to make out their words. Staring at the table full of food, but feeling too sick to eat.

That two such completely different realities could go on at the same time... was that life? Was there a secret somewhere in the middle?

When I looked over again at the service from my place alongside the hearse, I noticed the Deacon had finished and Aaron stood in front of the crowd, (every bit his Toast-Master graduate self, calmly and without any umms or uncomfortable pauses) and announced that the casket be lowered shortly.

Hispanic funerals almost always ended with the casket being lowered into the ground. This practice varied among cultures and individuals (and sometimes, with cemetery policy). White people generally left before the casket was lowered, and left the Funeral Director to be their witness. I always figured Hispanics were more comfortable with death. It was a huge part of their culture and they usually believed in Heaven.

I wondered if the young man whose body was in the casket was in Heaven. I wondered if I was going to go to Heaven.

The cemetery worker stepped forward and inserted a long metal key into the casket device.

At once, with a long, low moan and a slight shake as metal began to turn and move in protest to the new action; the casket shifted and began its slow descent into the earth below.

Like slow motion, the sister of the deceased boy leapt up from her chair. I saw her move out of the corner of my eye and turned my head towards her. Before anyone had a chance to register what was happening, the teenage girl threw herself at the descending casket and screamed in protest.

My eyes widened and I saw Aaron, Martin, and the cemetery worker all immediately move towards the casket to try to hold it in place. At the same moment, several men from the group of mourners ran up to retrieve the distraught girl. The entire crowd moved in on the heightening frenzy, many in the crowd now sobbing audibly. In those few seconds, we had lost control of the service.

I watched as the casket device began to shake and move dangerously over the open grave, angry with the weight of the new load and the unusual movement that the crowd created upon it, threatening to slip and topple them all into the grave.

Martin looked over at me in horror, but I was unable to penetrate the crowd that now surrounded all sides of the casket. The cemetery worker was displaced from his hold on the device and pushed back out of the way. He was yelling something, but his voice was lost in the agitation. Aaron still held on to his end of the casket, his face red and straining, the back seam of his charcoal grey suit jacket slowly pulling apart, his feet braced on the plank of wood on each side of the casket, (the planks that were now supporting the weight of the crowd).

I looked around for help and I saw the Deacon calmly removing his cassock while walking to his car.

It seemed like a dream. Everyone was crying and moving around, but silently. I mean, it must have been quiet; quiet enough that when the dead boy's Mother started screaming, it ripped through the crowd like a shotgun, stopping everyone in their place.

The entire crowd, Aaron, Martin, the cemetery worker still holding his long metal key—

We all just stood there while that boy's Mother howled out her anguish for her lost son. It didn't matter; English or Spanish, we all knew what she was saying, those primal, visceral, guttural wails. They came straight from her loins, the same loins that bore him into this world; the same loins that refused to accept the fact that he should not have gone first.

Slowly, one by one, the crowd began to move back from the casket, until I could see Martin and Aaron breathe in relief and try to regain composure. The girl who had thrown herself bodily on the casket was being led by several women back to the limo.

The boy's Mother howled her pain deep and long until I couldn't take the sound anymore. For some reason, I straightened my jacket, turned resolutely, and left the cemetery. I didn't even ask Aaron if I could. I just left. I walked like a robot— I rejected humanity.

I drove my van back to the little cream and brown mortuary.

Aaron and Martin pulled in shortly after. The three of us did not speak, but we did smile tiredly at each other and nodded in passing.

I watched as Aaron turned to go down the hall. I saw where the back of his jacket had ripped open when he was trying to hang onto the casket. I never have forgotten the sound that Momma made that day, but there was no time to ponder... while we were gone, two new cases had come in.

As I prepared my paperwork to meet with the four o'clock family, I wondered briefly what terrible beauty they would bring with them. I wondered if I would end up like Aaron one day, telling hopeful young apprentices that every family would take a little piece until there was nothing left while simultaneously spouting out Bible verses. And lastly, I wondered when I was going to get a raise.

After the arrangement, there would be paperwork to complete and bodies to embalm. I steeled myself for the work to come, but secretly I longed for the moment when I could go home, curl up with my little cat, and sleep.

CHAPTER 7

The night of the employee Christmas party I wore my best black dress and a pair of chandelier earrings with a lovely silver filigree design. I was so excited that I ran home after work to shower before the dinner. (After all, it was going to be my first time meeting the owner and I wanted to make a good impression.)

I sat in between Martin and Joel at the fancy French bistro and I anxiously watched the door for the elusive owner's appearance. A handsome young waiter with a perfectly straight spine set crystal glasses filled with ice water and lemon slices in front of us.

Joel raised one eyebrow and handed his water back to the waiter, "Throw this out and bring me back a gin."

"This is so fancy I don't know if I can behave myself..." Martin whispered to Joel and me jokingly.

Aaron stood up and cleared his throat. "I want to thank all of you for coming tonight to celebrate the birth of Jesus with your fellow employees. I would like to start off by saying that the owner of the mortuary extends his sincere apologies that he will not be able to join us tonight..."

I looked immediately at Martin in disappointment and he shrugged his shoulders at me in confusion.

"Please everyone join hands and let us pray," Aaron continued, bowing his head and taking his wife's hand on one side and Hank's wife's hand on the other. "Our Heavenly Father..."

✳ ✳ ✳

"I think he doesn't exist," Martin said as we stood outside the restaurant after the dinner was over.

Everyone else had already gone home to their families— except for those of us who didn't have families to go home to; me, Joel, and Martin.

"Who?" Joel asked, putting on his expensive looking coat.

"The owner," I answered, "Martin thinks the owner is some made up guy..."

"Like Charlie, from Charlie's Angels," Martin took a long, deep drag of his cigarette and blew smoke rings in my direction. "Now that was a good show. Although they kept switching one of the women around and I could never figure out why."

"Farah was the best one," Joel chimed in.

"No way," I said, "Tanya Roberts was the best one. She was the redhead. She was in that movie, the Beastmaster, too, remember that?"

Joel smiled and nodded, "I saw that movie, the one where they painted the tiger and the guy could talk to animals."

"Never trust redheads," Martin said seriously. "There is something wrong with every last one of 'em."

"You're so full of shit," I told him, laughing.

"I'm not kidding; it is a well known fact that all redheads have something wrong with them, like a chromosomal defect. Trust me on this," Martin said, holding his hands up as if taking a vow.

"Well, I'm going to go have another drink. Anyone want to go back to my place?" Joel asked, in a rare burst of outgoingness.

Afraid that the opportunity might never present itself again, I quickly agreed to join him. Perhaps the evening wouldn't be a total loss if I could get a little better understanding of this sad, strange little man who ran so far away from his home on the east coast. Truthfully, I was dying to see his apartment. I knew he lived a couple buildings over from mine, but this was the first time he breached formality and invited me over.

"Martin?" Joel asked.

Martin smashed out his cigarette on the sidewalk, "Sorry man, I still have to go back to work and embalm a case tonight."

After we said our goodbyes, Joel and I took our own cars home. I changed into jeans and walked over to his apartment.

His home was like I had expected— immaculate, clean, and modern. The furniture was sparse, but in very good taste. Too good, I thought, and for the first time I let myself realize that Joel was very probably gay. Grey and black dominated the color scheme. A footed sofa with silver and black vertical stripes sat next to matching curtains. I sat in one of two handsome leather chairs in solid black. The lampshades on either side of the couch had black fleur-de-lis prints on top of shiny silver material. Even the bathrobe that I could see barely peeking out from its hook on the back of the bathroom door was color coordinated. Soft music played from carefully camouflaged black speakers.

He mixed us golden drinks with rum in fancy glasses with silver etching around the rims. He served me first and then himself, every bit the gentleman. For some reason, I felt a little nervous. It wasn't the first time we had ever been alone, but it was the first time we had ever been alone outside of work.

"Gin is my drink of choice, but this special occasion calls for rum," Joel confided, sitting on the couch. He leaned forward to click his glass against mine and said in his sad, squeaky voice, "Cheers."

"Cheers." I sipped the powerful drink. "Tequila is my usual drink."

Joel raised his eyebrows and looked impressed, "Well, then you are my kind of girl."

I smiled and studied the glass my drink was in. It was delicate yet distinctly masculine, perfect for the cocktail it contained. Of course Joel would serve cocktails in the appropriate glassware. If I went through the drawers in his kitchen I would most likely find it filled with appropriate things; salad forks, dessert forks, matching cups and saucers, fine china for special occasions. All of the things that were easy to control were controlled quite impressively.

I started out using my best manners, but two lethal drinks later; we were both laughing and carefree, just about as friendly as a couple of drunks could be.

He took my glass and got up to fix us another round of those mind-altering cocktails.

"Well," Joel said, continuing our easy conversation, "before I went to Mortuary College, I was attending medical school."

"Really? I always knew you were smart," I said, browsing through his compact discs. My eyes immediately zeroed in on his Barbra Streisand disc. I casually glanced past it and noted a compilation of Andrew Lloyd Webber's love songs.

He smiled bashfully at my smart compliment. He had long since removed his jacket and tie and unbuttoned the top button on his dress shirt, looking more casual than I had ever seen him. I found him adorable on this night— with his straight well-groomed brown moustache and his cheeks all flushed from drink. For a moment, he almost acted like the young man that he was, instead of some crotchety old fart.

"So why are you a mortician instead of a doctor?"

He cracked ice cubes and looked thoughtful. I noticed that he was using fresh glasses instead of re-filling the old ones. I wondered if he had a germ fetish, but was too content to bother asking.

"A lot of things happened— my Mom got sick, I wasn't very disciplined so I couldn't keep up with my lessons," his voice lowered. "My Dad died."

"What was that last part?" I asked, looking up.

"My Dad died."

"Oh…" I swallowed and cleared my throat. "How old were you when that happened?"

"Twenty-two— still just a kid, really." He coughed. "I wasn't as independent as you are. I still lived with my parents." He walked over with our fresh drinks. "These drinks are very strong," he warned.

I was twenty-three, and I could not imagine losing my Mom. I sipped my drink. It was indeed very strong. "What are you trying to do, kill me?!" I teased.

"No way! You are my only friend." He finished his words with an uncomfortably solemn expression.

It really wrecked the fun mood we had going.

"So…" I said, trying my best not to grasp the intense loneliness in his last statement, "Tell me what happened after your Dad died?"

"Well, Mom wanted me to help her out a lot— handle things like the checkbook, yard-work, you know… stuff. So I did, of course. I was a good son and that is what I tried to be. You can't imagine what that was like." He took a long drink and then looked at me with a hard stare, his green eyes unyielding. "Pretty soon, I realized that she was killing me, too."

We stared at each other for a moment as the admission and its many meanings passed between us. My eyes were the first to drop.

"So that's when you came to California?" I finally managed.

"Well, that's when I became an alcoholic," he watched me curiously as he spoke, studying my reaction to discern if I was surprised at his extreme candor. "And then after that… I came to California."

"Oh," I said, looking down uncomfortably.

He laughed a loud, drunken laugh. "Ah... yes, Joel knows he is an alcoholic!" He slapped his knee vigorously. "I am not going to apologize. I deserve a vice. God bless alcohol!"

I raised my glass to toast to his.

"What a novelty," he said sadly, and smiled a wan smile. "Imagine! A Funeral Director who can't even deal with the death of his own Father! I have assisted hundreds of families through the death process, but who can help assist me through mine?!" He issued a strange laugh that was akin to a strangled cry.

If I had been sober, I might have felt uncomfortable listening as Joel went on about how he missed his Father and his life that should have been— he should have been a doctor, he should own a fancy home, he should have stood up to his Mother instead of running away.

I just watched him through the webby gauze of my drunken veil and drank him in. I became immersed in his reality— this gifted and haunted boy from the East Coast.

"So now let me ask you a question," Joel asked, becoming curiously steady.

"Shoot," I said, pleasantly studying a carved steel modern art piece that was on his coffee table that became suddenly more interesting now that I had a few drinks in me. It was abstract and I decided it was either meant to be a tree stump or a booger. I snickered to myself.

"What's going on with you and Martin? We have all been dying to know."

I burst out laughing. "Me and Martin?!"

"Just answer the question."

"Nothing," I said a bit too defensively. I stared at the metal art piece again. "Nothing romantic, I see that smile... you can wipe it off your face. We are just friends. He is old, I mean really old. Come on..."

Joel listened and nodded, keeping his small smile. He didn't believe a word I was saying and that really pissed me off.

"Don't look at me like that, all wise and shit." I scowled and sunk down sulkily in my chair, "You get me all drunk and then ask me about Martin. HA! Most of the time he drives me nuts! It's all I can do just to stand him..."

"Okay, okay already," Joel said. He rose to make himself another drink. "Jeez... I was just asking." He paused and then asked, "Is there anything you want to ask me?"

For a moment I actually considered just coming right out and asking him if he was gay. I think he might have wanted me to, but I just couldn't bring myself to do it. I didn't want to go too deep with Joel, something in me didn't want to know all of his secrets— I had a feeling the price would be steep. His world was fragile, full of shadows and fears, regrets and should-haves; heavy and dark, the curtains drawn and there was an IN door, but no way OUT. My own self-preservation instincts recoiled from going to that place with him. The thought of it made me feel a little sick to my stomach, and I could not explain quite why.

"Yes!" I shouted, "Yes, as a matter of fact there is..." I grabbed the metal art piece off the coffee table and held it up, "What in the hell is this supposed to be?!"

He laughed so hard he spilled rum as he poured. The golden liquid quickly beaded up on the counter.

Later on, I walked back to my building in the dark, my world spinning around me. My thoughts were thick with Joel and Martin and the mortuary, and finally my own loneliness, which always seemed more intolerable after I drank alcohol. I thought of how many nights Joel must have spent in that apartment, drinking alone. I knew I had been invited into a very private world.

People were so strange. It's like we were all woven out of this common thread. We had to be, or I wouldn't feel this unexplainable kinship to Joel, who sat day after day, drinking himself to death. He might just seem pitiful, if I couldn't feel his loneliness. And furthermore, where in the *hell* was the owner of the mortuary and why didn't he want to meet me?

I went up to the third floor and walked past my Mexican neighbors' open door and saw them inside, drinking and playing cards. I wondered if they realized how lucky they were to have a place where they belonged. Maybe one day they would invite me in.

To think that all these years went by—
starting out thinking every thought, every word
was special
until one day
you find out
you were only perfectly
adequate.

I didn't brush my teeth. I lie down on my bed next to Harold and fell asleep.

CHAPTER 8

Near the end of February, the owner bought a new Lincoln hearse. He had dropped it off in the middle of the night and taped the keys to the dry-erase board where we kept track of our active cases. The staff on the whole was very proud to drive it during funeral services. No other mortuary could compete with its elegance.

The hearse was jet black with chrome fixtures, a roll-out back deck with cherry wood paneling, automatic locks and windows, burgundy velvet curtains, and a switch that lowered or raised the back. The testosterone level rose to dizzying heights as the men of the mortuary stood around talking about cylinders and horsepower and blah, blah, blah...

A month after we acquired it, Martin and Joel accidentally locked themselves out of the hearse during a graveside service. It seemed they had gathered the family and instructed the pallbearers on the finer points of removing the casket from the hearse, the path they were to follow to the grave, and finally, how to place it carefully on the casket device.

However, things came to a complete standstill when Joel prepared to open the hearse to access the casket when he discovered the doors locked. At precisely the same moment, a horrified Martin noticed the keys still dangling inside the ignition.

Aaron came in to the lounge while I was at lunch and handed me the spare set of hearse keys. His face was red and he looked like he had been laughing. I looked up from my sandwich.

"Take these to the cemetery very quickly," he was hardly able to utter. "Martin and Joel locked the casket inside the hearse."

I tried to get myself under control during the short drive to the cemetery. I figured that as long as I did not look at Martin in the eyes, I wouldn't start laughing. I could only imagine what horrible shape Joel's underwear was in. I giggled all the way to the cemetery. It's a twisted life.

Soon I was driving up to the paved road that led to the gravesite. I lost my composure completely and my body became hunched over the steering wheel in laughter and anticipation.

Slowly the scene became visible over the hilly cemetery. Everyone stood on the side of the cemetery road— the family and friends, the stern-looking minister holding his Bible and looking at his watch, the regal ebony hearse with the white casket shining like a beacon inside, a strangely postured Martin, and finally— an obviously mortified Joel.

Martin absently patted his front shirt pocket. I bet he just couldn't wait to have a cigarette. I wiped away a tear and tried not to smile as I drew nearer.

I pulled in behind the flower van. Martin was already walking stiffly towards me. I rolled down my window and grinned sweetly.

There was an instant when I handed Martin the keys that our eyes met. A range of emotions ran across his face; embarrassment, mirth, pride, and anger. He would never stoop to beg for me to be merciful and let the incident pass without any smart comments. He would never give me the satisfaction of hearing him beg.

Neither one of us could muster a word. He glared at me with blazing eyes, nodded mechanically, and turned on his heel to head back to the hearse. A couple of mourners from the crowd clapped as he held up the keys.

I drove back to the mortuary, where Aaron and Hank were waiting for all the gory details. We all sat in the kitchen and had a good laugh over it.

About an hour later, I saw the flower van that Martin was in drive up on the security monitor. I smiled inwardly.

Martin appeared in the doorway shortly after, his jacket draped over his shoulder and his tie undone. Even his hair looked tousled.

"I hate you," he told me.

Martin and I laughed every time we saw each other for about a week over the incident.

Joel returned from the service reeking of alcohol, parked the new hearse sideways and half on the ice-plant in the front parking lot— and then he disappeared for the rest of the afternoon. He never discussed the incident again.

CHAPTER 9

Above all, we had to stand with a clear conscience. We aspired to raise arteries and conduct funerals and dress dead human bodies to the best of our ability. Our goal was to be able to replicate the appearance of good health and vigor by way of blush cosmetics and arterial dyes. These things were bigger than the words we spoke— and that is why we often spoke lightly.

Martin and I bantered back and forth all day long, but we both knew why we were there. More than anything, this bound us together as two Apprentices learning their trade. How could I account for it all?

Why did we all come to the mortuary to lay hands on the remnants of lives lost and those of their mourners? What calling brought us from all different ages and walks of life, to assemble in this place?

How could I explain to an outsider? That we could take a body that was ravaged by quick trauma or lingering disease, with brown spots and sunken eyes and fractures and dehydrated cheeks... and turn them into peaceful images in fresh clothing and contented expressions? This was the gift that we gave to our families. This was our contribution to this life.

It was impossible for me to account for it. Aaron would say it was God who compelled us. Martin would say it was to make a living. Joel would describe it as an endeavor of artistic expression. But, what good are words when used to describe passion?

All I know is that when I sat in with Martin on one of his first arrangements, his thirty-nine year old hands shook just as nervously as my twenty-four year old hands did. It made me smile when I saw that.

The same blood ran through all of us.

They could have fired me after I had sprayed my Supervising Embalmer in the face with the dirty preparation room hose and then crashed the van; they certainly could have. (I am quite sure that I would have made an able cashier at JC Penney's or even K-Mart.) But my life with the dead bodies was not meant to be over yet.

In fact, my life with the dead bodies was just beginning.

CHAPTER 10

I met with a middle aged woman to arrange the funeral for her husband, who died from liver cancer. She brought their teenage son, who sat away from us and would not speak. We both tried to draw him into the conversation and make him a part of the decision making process, but he was unable to participate. It was an exceptionally difficult arrangement.

At the appropriate moment, I led them both into the casket selection room. I explained the pricing system and various materials for interiors and exteriors. I heard my voice from far off somewhere as my eye caught the teenage boy wandering over to the women's casket wall. These were themed caskets with designs chosen to suit a woman's tastes; flowers, angels, doves, colored in pastels of pink, violet, and cream.

I stopped talking as I saw the freckled boy come to a halt in front of a white casket with pink roses painted on the lid and rounded, feminine corners. He pointed at it and looked at his Mom, with tears in his huge blue eyes.

His mouth opened, but no words came out. The woman went to him and squeezed her son's hand comfortingly.

She turned to me, "This is the one we want." Her voice wavered a little bit. "What do you think?" She stared at me without blinking, waiting for my answer.

"It reminds me of a jewelry box," I finally managed, not used to being drawn in to the decision making process.

She dabbed at the tears in her eyes and smiled at me bitter sweetly. "That's good," she said slowly, the words coming out in broken breaths, "because he was my jewel."

The son choked up when she said that and he abruptly left the casket display room, leaving me alone with the dead man's wife.

She stayed firmly where she stood and took my hand in hers.

"He can never be replaced, not for me…" she looked towards the door that her son had just exited from, "not for him."

My stomach tightened. I tried to think of what Aaron would say. The words came so easy for him. Her pain came off her in overwhelming waves and it was all I could do to just stand there, my Funeral Director training floated out of me and hung somewhere in space— lost.

"He was just diagnosed in December. Cancer is a terrible thing." She allowed tears to run freely down her pretty face. "He was too young to die."

"How long were you married?" I asked, my words finally landing in the right place. *Think, Louise, think, keep her talking about him*, Aaron's voice inside my head told me. The ironic part of me becoming a mortician is that it made me uncomfortable when people cried. (Don't try to figure it out... it doesn't make any sense. It is just another one of those crazy mysteries of life.)

"Twenty-three glorious years," she said wistfully.

"You don't see that much anymore," I said, wondering when it would be proper to lead her back into the arrangement room.

"I know, I know," she smiled softly. "We used to wonder why other couples didn't make it. We figured that they just didn't try hard enough, you know, didn't ever develop a friendship. Oh, we had such a wonderful time together..." she dabbed her eyes again with her tissue. "I think that is what I will miss most— he was my friend."

She took my hand into both of hers and squeezed it tightly, "I don't know if you are married or what, but I hope you get to experience that kind of closeness, even if just for one day."

I looked down at my hand inside of her perfectly manicured hold. "I hope so, too," my shaky, almost inaudible voice came out.

"I'm sorry I'm telling you all of this..." she apologized, letting go of my hand and turning so we could head back to the arrangement room. "You must hear this kind of thing all the time. Listen to me... I just keep talking and talking." She laughed a little and blew her nose.

"No, please don't apologize," I told her as we left the casket room, feeling a little sick. I had never known love like that, I thought. Maybe I never will. I was a twenty-four-year-old never-been-in-true-love stained-white-sweater-wearing mortician. It was completely depressing.

The dead man's wife appreciated things even after her true love was ripped from her unfairly, and she sat wishing such happiness on me. She was content with what her God had given her.

I was exhausted by the time the arrangement concluded. Every fiber in my wool slacks scratched and every second stung. The walls in the office seemed too white and my eyes squinted when I tried to fill out my forms.

After work, I went home and held Harold in my arms. She seemed happy to see me, but she really just wanted me to feed her. I popped the top on a can of Fancy Feast and scooped it onto a small blue plate and patted her on the head.

I realized that I was lonely, now more than ever (and I wasn't even drunk this time!) and I realized that things didn't really change— they just went around and around.

Some days on the job were more difficult than others.

CHAPTER 11

On the last day of March, the breaking apart of Joel commenced. I suppose we all knew it would come eventually. Or maybe we just didn't want to get too involved. Maybe we were just consumed in our own narcissistic miasmas. I made myself up pathetic excuses like: *I am not in charge around here; it's not for me to interfere.* I am sure we all had our own rationale for looking the other way. I wish I could have been a better friend to him.

It all started when Joel had driven the van to a local doctor's office to pick up a signed death certificate.

We were busy that day. Martin and I were dressing bodies in the preparation room. Hank was washing the hearse to go on a graveside service.

Aaron was off that day, (which incidentally always seemed to coincide with Joel coming into work particularly inebriated.)

Lisa, the front office receptionist, came bursting through the preparation room doors with a worried look on her thin face. Lisa was a wink under five feet tall and wore her modern skirts short and cleaned her impressive amount of jewelry every morning with a toothbrush to make it sparkle. Every morning she made a package of flavored instant oatmeal in a coffee cup heated in the microwave with enough water to make it the consistency of thick soup, and ate it while we discussed the new cases.

I had been applying lipstick to a dead woman's lips with a tiny brush and Martin was working pantyhose up the legs of another dead woman.

We both looked up.

"What's with you?" Martin asked her, without missing a beat, "You look like someone is holding a small turd under your nose."

I smiled at Martin's observation, continuing my lip application, rounding out the Cupid's bow (the upper crest of the top lip), just like I learned in school.

"Dr. Lee's office just called and his nurse said that the death certificate is signed and ready to be picked up," she reported worriedly.

"So what is the problem?" I asked pointedly.

Lisa stamped her tiny heels on the hard terrazzo floor, making small angry clacking noises to display her frustration. "That is the D.C. I sent Joel on... I need it for Hank's graveside."

Without a Death Certificate that was signed by a physician and Burial Permit filed by the County, burial could not take place. Things sometimes happened last minute, due mainly to the doctor's cooperation with responding to our faxes requested cause of death and then the doctor's availability for a signature on an original that Lisa would type in to complete.

"How long ago did Joel leave?" I asked, feeling a knot of bad omen beginning to tighten in my stomach.

"He's been gone two hours."

"Here we go..." Martin sighed.

We knew something was wrong with Joel when he came in that morning. Mornings were generally hard on him, but he was in an extra foul mood that day. Joel even put aside his usual territorialism over the preparation room work and passed off the dressing and casketing of two bodies to Martin and me.

"I'm going to call his house," I said, removing my latex gloves and untying my white lab coat.

"You think he's there?" Martin asked.

I shrugged, "Maybe. Where else would he go?" I prayed that Joel was not sitting at home, getting plastered. I was opting for something less incriminating, like a simple car crash with a few minor injuries.

"Even if he was at home, he wouldn't be stupid enough to answer the phone," Martin said logically, even as he and Lisa followed behind me to the phone that was in the lounge.

I grabbed the staff roster off the bulletin board and dialed Joel's number, still praying that Joel maybe just had a seizure and passed out behind the In-n-out burger.

A very drunk Joel answered the phone, his voice thick and slow.

"Joel, its Louise."

"Oh... Lou," he slurred. "I'm so glaaad you called me. You're my only friend. You are my blest friend."

"What are you doing at home, buddy?" I asked. Martin and Lisa watched me expectantly, mouthing questions about Joel's state.

"Is he drunk?" Lisa whispered, pulling lightly on my arm.

Joel was busy chattering away. I covered the mouthpiece. "He's wasted," I told her.

Martin ran a hand through his well-groomed hair. He was still wearing his lab coat (a real no-no in the lounge— Aaron would have been furious if he was there).

"Louuuuu-Louuuu," Joel's happy chatter turned into a long moan. "I had to come home. I couldn't— I jes' couldn't take it anymore. I'm at home now... remember when you clame over that trime? Of course you remember... I went there..."

"Where is the van?" I asked. "I'm sending someone over to pick it up." I pointed at Martin.

Martin began shaking his head and waving his hands. "I have a family coming in to finalize," he said, "I can't leave now."

At the same time, I heard Joel's voice on the receiver. "The van... the van..." he laughed, "Oh yeah, that's here, too. I'll bring it black..." I heard him rattling keys in the background.

"NO!" I said loudly. "Joel, you don't have to do that. The last thing we need right now is you driving anywhere. You just stay right where you are."

Joel's voice changed instantly from giggles to loud sobs, "You care 'bout me..." he cried pitifully. "I knew you cared..."

"We all care about you, Joel," I said into the phone. Martin rolled his eyes and Lisa pinched him. "I am sending Martin right over. Just wait there, okay?"

I could hear Joel moving things around and at one point drop something and curse loudly.

Martin was tugging on my sleeve. "I told you I can't go," he said between tugs.

I heard a bunch of rustling around on the line. I heard the sound of his ice cube tray cracking and ice clinking against a glass— one of his fancy glasses with silver etching around the rim. The sound of it made me sad.

"Joel!" I said loudly. "Stay there, okay?"

"Okay Lou," he said.

I hung up the phone.

"I can't go get the van. I have to casket this guy before my family comes back in to finalize," Martin said matter-of-factly.

"I never thought he would go this far," Lisa said, shaking her head.

I looked at my wristwatch. "Man, none of us have time to go get the van. I would say leave it there, but we need both van for services this afternoon," I wrinkled my brow, "Why did he have to do this today of all days?" I felt the tension begin to rise in my stomach. An image began to form in my mind— me, standing between my loyalty to Joel and my loyalty to being a mortician. Being a mortician won hands down. I reached for the phone.

"What are you doing?" Lisa asked. "Are you calling him again?"

"I'm calling Aaron," I declared, flipping through the employee rolodex, cradling the phone between my shoulder and ear.

"Wait a minute there, sister," Martin said firmly, and I was surprised to feel his hand over mine on the rolodex. "Let's just talk about this first."

I put the phone back on its cradle, and turned to face him and a concerned looking Lisa. "Talk about what? We are swamped and Joel is out there getting drunk with the company vehicle! Aaron needs to come in and handle this. This is bigger than us right now. This is why Aaron makes the big bucks."

"But you are taking fate into your own hands..." Martin argued.

"What in the hell is that supposed to mean?" I asked pointedly. The whole situation was growing increasingly frustrating to me. I looked at my watch again. I thought of the bodies waiting for us in the preparation room, the service this afternoon that now had no flower van, the Death Certificate waiting at a doctor's office in the next city that we needed to file for burial that afternoon. There was no way we would make it, I thought. I grabbed a piece of hair and started chewing it nervously.

"Aaron will fire him, Louise."

I looked at Martin, "That is not my problem," but I felt myself setting the Rolodex back on the counter. "He should have thought of that before he pulled this stunt," I added, though my voice sounded weaker.

"Joel has really serious emotional issues..." Lisa said, bringing a perfectly manicured hand up to her chin thoughtfully, "maybe right now if we showed him that somebody cares about him, it would plant the seed that helps turn him around."

I snickered, my cynicism revealed. I stopped when Lisa shot me a look of disappointment.

"The way I figure it is that everyone deserves one screw-up," Martin said.

"Well, should we take a vote?" I asked sarcastically, "Where's Hank? I'll betcha it's a tie..." I turned my gaze on Martin. "And since when are you so forgiving? You would kick my ass if I even thought about pulling a stunt like this... and on such a day!"

"We're different than Joel," he stated simply.

Lisa was wearing her maternal expression, the one she usually saved for when she was telling us about one of her Pastor's sermons and how it changed her life. "I really think we can help him. He needs us now," she said softly, almost pleadingly.

We all just stood there in silence for a little while. I stared at the ground.

I finally pushed the Rolodex further away from me and leaned against the counter. I was so pathetic. I could feel myself cave under the pressure. "Fine, you guys do whatever you want. Tomorrow you can tell Aaron we donated the van to a local charity that helps alcoholics." I sounded mean. Weak people usually sound mean like that.

"You know," Martin confided, "somebody gave me a second chance when I was drinking real heavy. I never forgot that."

I shook my head in disbelief, "Do you honestly think that this won't happen again with Joel? Come on, he's been getting worse and worse. Maybe if we turn him in for this Aaron and the owner will offer him rehab instead of firing him..."

They both just stood there and watched as I began to list off the advantages of calling Aaron and why it was so unfair for Joel to put us in this position. I became madder and more stressed with every second that passed with the body that I had been working on in the preparation room still not getting any closer to being ready for her afternoon viewing. I was angry with Aaron most of all, because he must have known that Joel needed help, that he was getting worse. I thought of all the times Joel came in smelling like a walking distillery... Aaron must have known...

The three of us were still in a circle debating what should be done when Joel stumbled into the room with the van keys dangling from his pinky finger.

"I brought these for you because you were so nice to me..." Joel said, holding the keys out to me. He swayed drunkenly and smiled sweetly.

We all stared at him in disbelief. Lisa's mouth fell open slightly.

Joel looked awful. His eyes were bloodshot and glazed, unable to focus on anything in particular as they moved slowly back and forth while his body swayed in an imaginary wind. His face appeared flushed pink and looked greasy. I noticed that his tie, however, was still tied neatly into its perfect Double Windsor.

It is possible for someone to be dead even though they were still alive, I thought, feeling sick to my stomach, that same familiar nausea. I turned to leave as Martin began asking Joel questions about how he drove in his condition. I could hear Lisa speaking motherly and ministering in her soft, comforting voice.

I trudged back to the preparation room and stopped, gazing over the dead bodies lying on stainless steel tables in various stages of dress. We took such pains to close their eyelids and secure their mouths closed. Nobody could deliver Joel that kind of peace in this world. It was too much, and we didn't have time for any of it in our little cream and brown mortuary that day.

"Too much death around here," I muttered sarcastically to Martin, who appeared quietly in the doorway.

The second my eyes met his concerned gaze, they started to fill with tears. I turned my head so he wouldn't see and pretended to be absorbed with putting my gloves back on.

"I'm not crying, you know," I lied.

"I know," Martin said in a voice I had never heard him use before. It was a soft voice, unfamiliar.

When I heard that voice, I choked up even more.

"Hey Lou," Martin said, his voice brightening. He pointed at the dead man on the table closest to him, chosen at random, "This guy died? I didn't even know he was sick!" He said, repeating an old line we often used in the preparation room late at night so we could lighten the mood.

It was a joke that made me smile the other hundreds of times he'd used it. He waited for me to look at him with his big smile on his face. When he saw my sad face, his grin faded away.

With nothing more to say and a huge amount of work still ahead of us, we went quietly about our business.

CHAPTER 12

The next day, our little mortuary buzzed along like nothing had ever happened. Lisa ate her soupy oatmeal out of her coffee cup and chatted, Martin drank his coffee and browsed the obituaries for copies of his latest, Hank busied himself with the sports section, Joel looked over the arrangements on the board and made notes, and I perused the Horoscopes absently, my stomach in knots.

It was just like any other day.

It was utterly without climax. The casualness of it ate away at me.

Looking for some kind of recognition was pointless. Our silence was merely buying Joel another drunken day on the job. I sat quietly, but my mind was screaming and restless. I looked at Joel, then Martin, each consumed with their own morning ritual; each no more bothered with the events of the day before than the other; each at peace... unlike me.

I wondered why Martin and Lisa had hope for Joel, and I, who was probably the closest to him, had none. Maybe I was a horrible person, two-faced, cold. Aaron would say it was because I hadn't found God yet. I was so sick of feeling judgment from Aaron's God.

I just wanted to be a good Funeral Director. Why couldn't it just be that simple? Why did I feel like I was waiting for the roof to fall in?

If I would have known the outcome of those days, or if I have had a hint as to what the future might bring, I might have been able to unclench the knot that seemed to form permanently in my stomach. (But life was not nearly so kind.)

We had bought Joel a little more time. Maybe Martin and Lisa were right. Perhaps Joel would take this opportunity to turn himself around...

It could happen.

That night I snuggled with Harold under the covers in my little apartment that I paid for all by myself. By all outside appearances, I was getting along just fine in life.

The Mexican neighbors who lived a couple doors down were blasting music and the heavy bass vibrated through the floors. My Grandma on my Dad's side was Mexican. That is where I got the trademark round nose. My Mom had one of those long, elegant, pointy noses... the kind I always wished I had. But no, I was stuck with the "cute" little round nose. A nose like that could hardly fit in with the cool sophisticated woman I wanted to be, the kind with the regal profile and high arching eyebrows.

I suppose it was loneliness that made me consider going over to hang out with my loud neighbors. I could march right over there and tell them that I was a Mexican, too. I could sit with them drinking forty ouncers in their crisp white t-shirts and khakis and winos, and for a moment I could feel like I fit in someplace. But here I was stuck between Mexican, English, and Polish; not enough of any one thing to fit into anywhere.

I looked at the clock next to my bed. Harold meowed in irritation when I moved slightly. It was late. The cops would be coming soon to tell the Mexicans to quiet down. I would hear their voices in the hall, muffled and authoritative.

I wondered if those Mexicans ever noticed me. I wondered if they knew I was there, and that my Grandma was Mexican. I wondered if they thought about the life inside of my apartment the way I wondered about theirs. I guessed probably not.

Harold's eyes were closed and she had that look of total contentment that cats get when they are sleeping on you and they know that you won't disturb them by getting up even if you have to go the bathroom really bad. She started purring— she knew that I was admiring her.

I waited until I heard the cops knocking on my neighbor's door before I fell asleep.

❊ ❊ ❊

That night Martin and I went out to dinner. Eating was what we did together. If we were not eating, we were discussing what we were going to eat, or where we would eat, or things we had eaten in the past. I can recall entire conversations between us on our car phones coming back from different funeral services where the only information exchanged was what we had eaten for dinner the night before. The day Martin discovered the broiler in his oven worked better if he left the oven door cracked open we talked for two hours about a variety of other well and not-so-well-known food preparation tips.

We were most certainly replacing food for some vital component that we both lacked, but since we were similar in our dysfunction— we didn't attempt to fix each other; and we did have some great meals.

The conversation flowed at its smoothest when food was in between us. Martin never seemed to mind when I jumped around from subjects like God to pondering what I might look like with bangs.

He listened to all my chatter with gracious attention. Usually, he had a cigarette in one hand and a cup of coffee in the other. He would just sit back in his chair looking like a man who had all the time in the world and smile or frown in the appropriate places in my dialogue. He would offer me sound advice like, "Families come first; we have to make that our mission statement when we buy our own mortuary," to "I like your bangs much better long."

Set a table for two, pile a stack of pancakes on it, and we were pretty much set for the night.

But that night was different. It was almost... somber. We both sat in the brown vinyl booth in the Spire's down the street from the mortuary looking rather defeated.

The people sitting in the booth behind us were discussing the high cost of funerals (it was uncanny how often we heard people discussing funerals at restaurants.) We listened to them try to advise each other, filled with the standard myths and misconceptions. The words 'chiselers,' 'hustlers,' and 'just throw me a box and burn me,' came up of course.

Martin smiled at me as they loudly traded stories of funeral service foul-ups and how one of them single-handedly stopped a mortician from robbing his family blind.

"You should throw your business card over there," Martin told me, throwing a sideways glance at their booth.

I was playing with my silverware, it was this nervous habit I had. "I dare you to walk over there and give them yours," I said, more to my spoon than to him.

"I would if I felt like," Martin lied. "You, on the other hand, don't have the balls."

I feigned outrage. "I don't have any balls!"

He laughed.

We listened to some more of their conversation in silence. He drank a sip of his coffee. I made a small catapult with my knife and spoon which I used to promptly fire my straw wrapper at Martin. It struck him in the chest; a direct hit. I felt the small glory as he narrowed his eyes at me, then I let out a big sigh and felt sad again.

"You know I hate it when you are depressed." He told me. "I am going to have to honk you on the nose if you don't snap out of it."

"Do you think you could just go easy on me tonight? I'm not in the mood."

"What joy would I have in my life if I could not pick on you?"

I raised my eyebrow at him. "It is absurd that you are older than me. Emotionally, I am far superior."

"That is probably true."

I regarded him suspiciously, waiting for the slam which would surely follow.

"I believe that a beautiful woman should be put up on a pedestal…" he said, looking gravely serious, "just up high enough so that you can see up her dress."

I smiled half-heartedly. "Martin, I am actually serious for once. I just don't feel like playing the bullshit game tonight." I rubbed my head. It felt heavy.

"Fine then, Miss fussy-pants."

Our food came. I had a hamburger. Martin had meatloaf. The waitress had blonde hair with dark roots and a wide derriere that caught Martin's approving eye.

"Sicko," I commented to him as he watched her walk away.

"You gonna eat your pickle?" He asked, eyeing my plate hungrily.

I shook my head and the pickle changed hands.

"Hey, Martin?"

"Yeah?"

"Do you ever think about embalming me?"

He ate a huge piece a meatloaf and mashed potatoes and answered with his mouth full, "Sometimes when you're acting really naughty."

"I'm serious."

"So am I."

I put down my burger. "I would probably get really good fluid distribution."

"Probably. You're young and healthy. Me, on the other hand…" he chuckled to himself. "You know that my arteries are shot… filled with crud."

I agreed. "I can picture what your arteries would look like," I said, staring at his neck.

"I want you to know that conversations like this are the reason that neither one of us are dating," Martin stated, raising his fork at me.

We ate for a little while in silence. The waitress with the generous rear brought me another soda and Martin watched her walk away again.

"Your arteries are probably sclerotic from all that white-trash crap you eat," I snickered under my breath.

"It's sad but true. You'll have a heck of a time embalming me. Are you going to eat all of your fries?"

I pushed some of my fries onto his plate. "When I think about Joel, I just can't believe it. I mean, on the inside... we are all just a mess of vasculature..."

"Are you trying to figure out what makes us human again?" He reached over to grab the ketchup, but instead swung right and honked me on the nose.

I waved his long arm away. "I just don't understand how just a couple of centimeters deep, we all look the same... and then somewhere on the way out, we all become so different. I just don't understand life anymore." I watched him for any signs of comprehension.

He had his head down, busy eating.

The conversation flowed over again from the booth behind us. They were talking about some guy who had recently been arrested for selling burial plots to more than one person.

I set the last part of my burger down with a sigh and pushed my plate away a little.

Martin finally looked up. "Hey, are you okay?" He stopped chewing and put his fork down, looking immediately consoling. "I'm sorry, Lou. I'll think about embalming you, okay? I'll think about it."

The world seemed to close in around our tiny booth.

"Hey sister," he said, "Don't let this thing with Joel get to you. I know what you're saying— I just don't know how to say it like you do. I feel all of the same things you do." He searched for something else to say, "Did I tell you how cute you look tonight?"

"No," I said quietly.

"Well, you do look really cute tonight. I should have said it earlier." His gaze ran across my face and down to my blouse that was the color of red wine. "That color makes you look radiant."

I blushed and couldn't help smiling the tiniest smile.

The world exhaled and was content to move back from us a bit. I was momentarily lost in the gauzy haze of a good compliment. The familiar sounds of restaurant rumble filled with muffled conversations and clinking dishes eased back into my reality.

"My Mom gave me this barrette. It's from Jamaica," I offered, touching the small silver piece in my hair.

His face lit up, making him look handsome. "My dear, it looks lovely. In fact, I cannot recall having ever seen a shinier head of ebony black hair."

I smiled and thought of Martin's signature line that he had repeated to me too many times to count, *If you can't dazzle 'em with your intelligence, than baffle 'em with your bullshit.'* I knew this was probably the bullshit, but it was all the same to me; and it just so happens that a

good compliment could usually get me out of the worst
of moods for a little while.

And I was sick of being sad tonight.

Pride goes before a fall echoed Aaron's warning
voice in my head. I quickly waved it away.

It was hard for me to believe that Martin felt all the
same things I did, even though he kept insisting that I
was the voice of his inner thoughts. He certainly wore
life more comfortably than I did.

Was he lonely, too? Was he scared? Did he get
bored with his look and wonder what he would look like
with a different hairstyle?

I smiled to myself as I watched him sitting across
from me, trying to make me laugh in order to ease his
own burdens; eating off my plate— somehow innately
aware of the slightest hint of my distress—and
incidentally, my monthly bill.

I thought at that moment that I loved him. It didn't
make any sense, but somehow, I needed him.

His one-liners were well known. His comedic timing
was impeccable. And while he was quite entertaining
(and most people loved to laugh at a fool)—

I found his antics full of grace,

his laughter full of understanding,

his rambling reminiscences completely whole and
without malice,

his pride at provoking all of the employees into fits of
laughter inspiring—

Maybe everything would be all right.

CHAPTER 13

June brought on sunny skies and cool breezes. The death rate dropped, and Hank told me that summer months were generally slow. We got to go home on time most days. Martin and I had time to go to movies and play horseshoes at the park together. Sometimes I went for several days without touching a dead body.

The break in cases gave the staff plenty of time to do the things for the mortuary that we neglected during the busy winter months. We shampooed the carpets, detailed the vans and hearses, and moved caskets around in the selection room. Martin and I spent as much time outside as possible beneath the warm sun— picking chores that took a long time, but didn't require much thought.

They were enjoyable days. I had been at the mortuary for a year, half of my apprenticeship and fifty embalmed bodies were under my belt. I could finally see the light at the end of the tunnel.

Even Joel seemed happier. He walked around fluffing the pillows on the lobby couches and spraying

Lysol. I didn't notice him disappearing and then come back smelling like liquor. He chatted with us, and once even offered a clumsy apology for his stunt with the hearse. It made me feel happy and secure, like everything might work out just fine after all.

The staff was outside in the back carport on one of the most sweltering of days. We hadn't had a first call in six nights. Martin and I had just finished vacuuming out the hearse. We relaxed by leaning up against the building in the shade with Hank and Joel, followed shortly by Lisa, who had seen us sitting back there in the security monitor in the front office and decided to join us. She propped the back door open so she could still hear the phone if it rang.

Martin lit up a cigarette. Everyone but Hank (who relaxed with his eyes shut) watched him smoke it. People always watched Martin smoke— like they were hypnotized. The delicate tendrils of smoke drifted past his thin lips and up into the atmosphere until they blended with the sky above. I watched the smoke until I could not see it anymore.

Lisa watched him for a little while and then chided him. "Uh-oh, Martin's finished vacuuming the hearse... better have a cigarette."

She often ribbed Martin about how he had to have a cigarette after he finished anything— making arrangements, going on services, or embalming.

"You know it, baby," Martin agreed, closing his eyes behind his sunglasses.

"That cigarette is going to kill you someday," Joel said dryly.

Martin opened one eye to look at Joel and replied, "I hear it takes ten years off your life… but it's the last ten and they suck anyway." He threw a quick wink in my direction before he closed his eye again.

"But isn't it strange how he smokes after every little thing?" Lisa continued.

Martin looked thoughtful for a moment, "I have often wondered what people do after sex if they don't smoke…"

"We eat popsicles," I piped up, which earned a smirk from Hank.

"Hey, that sounds good!" Lisa said excitedly. "Let's have someone go get us all popsicles."

We all smiled. Aaron went home early for the day and we had the place to ourselves.

"I'll go," Joel said, with an unfamiliar, good-natured look on his face. "I'll even pay."

The employees of the cream and brown mortuary spent the rest of the afternoon in the shade with our jackets cast over the backs of office chairs, eating popsicles and teasing each other about the way we ate them. By the time the week was over, the mortuary was spotless, the cars were stunning, and we seemed closer as a staff.

Through it all, Martin and I were best friends. We never got too close. We hardly touched. We tried not to linger in doorways or stay too long in the car once it stopped. And we behaved.

(But my eyes devoured him when he was not watching.)

CHAPTER 14

Joel invited me to his house for dinner on a Saturday.
A friend of his from back East was in town and he
insisted that I meet him. I was a little hesitant to
immerse myself in his reality again, feeling like I had
finally fully recovered from the last episode, but his
sincerity and childlike joy over the possibility that I
would meet one of his childhood friends won me over.

When Joel was happy, possibilities seemed to open
up around us. When Joel was happy, bodies got dressed
to perfection— birds sang and everyone got along. The
world was right.

Joel himself was intoxicating, and he drank to dilute
his own essence, for nothing as fragile as his glass
menagerie could last.

I walked over to his apartment after work. An
inebriated Joel opened the door and pulled me in by my
arm.

I made my way past the door frame and noticed a
small boyish-looking man with white skin and hair
blacker than mine sitting at Joel's table. He had his leg

crossed at the thigh and he turned to regard me with interest, although not exactly warmly. He was handsome, in a soft way, with pert features and dark, knowing eyes.

He set his drink aside and rose gracefully from the table and sashayed unhurried over to me. He presented me with one perfect hand that had obviously never known manual labor. I tentatively shook it, curling my fingers under in an attempt to hide my short, unpolished nails. I silently obsessed over how rough my hand must have felt in his.

His strong dark eyes traveled from my face to my feet and back again before he finally smiled with his full, overly-sensual lips.

Joel gushed over the both of us as I went through the silent examination his friend was giving me. His name was Miles, they had gone through school together, and he had come to visit California for reasons that were too obscure for me to understand... Joel went on and on about his friend... he was a Scorpio (so he packed a punch), he had gotten kicked out of college for smoking pot in class, he was renowned in the greater Scranton area for his piano playing abilities...

All the while, Miles's eyes never moved from mine, as if he was testing me somehow. I stared straight back at him, determined to show him that I could not be intimidated. I honestly wasn't sure what we were vying over, but I had always been one who enjoyed a worthy opponent nonetheless.

Finally, Miles broke eye contact and very respectfully offered me the chair next to him at the glass dining table. Joel began fiddling around in the kitchen and before I knew it, a shot of Don Julio Silver Tequila was in front of me with a bright green lime wedge hanging onto the rim.

I laughed and let out a sigh.

Joel slapped me on the back affectionately, something I could not remember him doing before that night. "You said Tequila is your drink of choice, right?" He set the bottle of Don Julio before me. "Only the best."

I nodded my head and took the drink in hand, genuinely touched by the expensive gesture and the thought behind it, "You are too good to me..."

Miles picked up his drink and held it smartly as he said in his perfectly annunciated, resonant voice, "To old friends, and to new friends." His dark eyes burrowed into mine and in that moment, we formed an understanding. I understood that Joel was his rightful property— and he understood that I meant no harm to his rightful property.

Well, here's to another page in my journal, I thought as I raised my glass.

My life with my Mom prepared me for this night. She was an art broker and owned several art galleries through the years as I was growing up. Artists, gays, and gay artists decorated my adolescent life. Their protected world, as Mom had explained to me so long ago, was entered only by invitation, and guarded closely against those who meant harm. Mom explained that once you were in, you were offered care and warmth that was not present in other people's lives; and that genetic kinship was not necessary to form a family. They basically had to create their own realities in which they could survive, and that was why it was so sacred to them. Gay men would tend each other straight through to the deathbed, even after all the others had disappeared— and when they decided they loved you, they loved you forever.

I touched my small glass to Miles's large glass. He looked at me knowingly. His eyes told me everything. *Yes, Joel was gay. Yes, I was welcome.* (But only because Miles approved it). *Yes, I will tell you all you want to know.* His eyes promised the secret past that Joel would not tell... the pain, the compulsion, and the sexual truth that he could not bear. It was an old understanding between the two of them; one that had been unconsciously agreed to long before I had stumbled upon them. I was a guest here, and I knew it.

I was intrigued by the possibilities of the night that would ensue.

Joel began to set serving dishes on the table before us: a small platter with filet of salmon in a cream sauce, grilled asparagus, a salad of baby greens with aged sherry dressing, and a steaming loaf of crusty bread. Everything looked and tasted exquisite.

Now it should be known that I had always had a propensity towards gluttony, so I took the opportunity to eat to the point of pain. I was pretty sure that I had lived a past life where I was starved to death, because in this life, I was ravenous.

Joel continued to bring me shots of Tequila, each one in a new glass, of course; and he mixed Gin and Tonics for him and Miles. I noticed that Joel showed off for Miles, trying to gain his favor about the life he made for himself in California. I offered Miles some tidbits of

Joel's marvelous mortuary work, which pleased Joel to no end.

As the dinner disappeared, our level of intoxication grew and our familiarity increased. The small apartment was now alive with music, our loud laughter, and drunken dialogue.

Joel was explaining some of the finer points of Restorative Art to Miles. Restorative Art is the term mortician's use for any reconstructive or makeup work we performed on the dead bodies.

I smiled to myself as Joel took on his usual snobbish, semi-patronizing personae that he used when he was teaching Martin and me. In my inebriated state, it seemed funny, and a little sad. I lost my smile as quickly as it came.

Miles looked un-impressed. "I heard you put something like chicken wire in their mouths to keep them closed. Ewww… gross." He waved his hand and took a drink.

Joel looked offended. He narrowed his bloodshot eyes. "That's a lie," he snapped, almost losing his balance on his chair. "We carefully secure the jaw with a needle-injector, or with suture. Isn't that right, Louise?" He spoke louder than he probably intended as his irritation rose.

I had gotten up from the table and was on my way to the couch with my Tequila glass in hand. "Yep. That's right."

Miles got up and followed me, arranging himself pertly into the black leather chair that I had sat in last time I was at Joel's apartment. Miles continued to press Joel without even glancing his way, "I heard that you take out the eyes and replace them with styrofoam balls. The guts, too. Then you fill up the body with sawdust and spray perfume on it." And with that, Miles shot me a naughty smile and winked.

Joel jumped up from the table, now fully enraged. Miles sat completely unruffled on his chair and sipped his cocktail. Joel began to clear the dishes from the table and yell at Miles simultaneously. "You…" Joel screamed viciously to the back of Miles's coiffed head, "have NO idea what it is that we trained Embalmers do! Good grief, No! That is so stupid. We don't take anybody's guts out! What would we do that for?" Joel had a little trouble walking straight in his condition and he slammed hard into the counter with his stack of dirty dishes.

I sat in my place on the couch, looking at that weird metal sculpture on Joel's coffee table and wondered why Joel didn't have a cat. Cats made great pets.

Miles shrugged and waved his hand backwards as if dismissing Joel. "He has always been too easy to torment, the drunken bastard," Miles whispered cutely to me while grinning with satisfaction.

I smiled and glanced at Joel. He was trying to blow out the candles on the dinner table and wasn't having much luck. He kept swaying and blowing and then accidentally knocked one over and cursed loudly as he slapped it out.

I laughed and turned back to the sculpture. I began to see a figure forming in the metal. I blinked my eyes to try to clear my slight double vision.

"You will never have any idea the patience and skill that it takes to reconstruct a nose or an ear that has been torn off or disfigured by disease. I have practiced years to get to where I am today... I am the best there is. Louise knows..." Joel pointed at me with an unsteady finger.

"He's the best at our mortuary," I said to Miles, who merely shrugged like he was bored.

Joel pointed to Miles, "YOU don't understand the kind of pressure that is put on you during a service! You have never had to work a day in your life!"

Miles leaned over to me and whispered, "That's because I am worth it." He smiled like a Cheshire cat and sat back into the leather.

Joel went on, "There are no mistakes allowed! No chance for do-over's! You don't even know what it means to have someone count on you like that..."

Miles looked at me and raised a knowing eyebrow, unperturbed by Joel's attack.

I jerked my gaze away from the sculpture when I heard Joel break a glass in the sink. Miles didn't even blink. Joel was cursing himself and wrapping a paper towel around a bloody finger.

"Oh man," I said, standing up, "Are you okay?"

Joel waved me off, "Of course I am okay," he said testily in my direction. "Wait a minute..." he stopped suddenly and then leered drunkenly, "I know how to prove to you what Embalmers do!" And he stumbled off towards the bedroom.

"That's right, you drunk prick, take yourself to bed!" Miles called after him. Then he laughed and turned back to me. "He always was a bitchy drunk."

We heard drawers opening and closing loudly from the bedroom.

"What do you think he is doing in there?" I asked Miles, sipping my drink.

"Awww... who cares?" He asked, waving his perfect white hand again. He leaned closer to me and bored down on me with his huge dark eyes. His black eyelashes seemed a mile long.

"So he has always been like this?" I asked.

"Since his Dad died." He wrinkled in upturned nose in thought. "He drinks too much, he freaks out, you know... the usual."

My interest perked up. "You were around when his Dad died?" I asked, leaning forward.

"Of course. His parents and mine were longtime friends." He leveled his gaze on me, "Don't get me wrong, he was pretty screwed up before his Dad died, too. You can thank his Momma for that."

"What is his Mom like?" I asked, trying to lower my voice so Joel wouldn't hear us from the other room.

Miles let out his breath as if the mere thought of her exhausted him. "Oh Lord, where to begin? Very controlling... He could never do anything right. I think she was even jealous of me at one point, the bitch." He let out a small snort and took another drink before continuing. "She made him enroll in the seminary at one point. She wanted him to be a priest, the old hag. Boy, did she have her wires crossed!"

"Is that before he went to Medical School?" I asked curiously.

He laughed. "Medical School? Is that what he told you? Well, I'm not surprised," Miles leaned back and sighed. "In his dreams... maybe. He was going to be a priest, just like Momma wanted. He almost made it, too.

It's like that book about men that says that the son has to take the key from under his Momma's pillow... well, Joel never got his hands on that key."

My stomach started to feel a little sick. I looked at my Tequila glass and set it down on the coffee table, pushing it away from me. Suddenly, I felt like I had enough to drink.

Miles's clear voice rang into and out of my consciousness as I reeled with this new information.

"Is that why Joel came to California?" I asked.

Miles was surprisingly composed for having consumed so much alcohol. His voice was smooth and steady, and his eyes were still quick and alert. "Joel came to California because his lover kicked him out for drinking too much..."

I stared at the metal sculpture as I listened to Miles's lackadaisical recap of Joel's troubled life. The form of the crude metal sculpture began to materialize into two bodies that were tangled into one another. I squinted my eyes and tried to make out where one left off and the other began, but it was not possible. The entire sculpture upset me, I realized. It was confusing and made me unsure.

Everything inside began to scream for me to get up and get out of there before Joel came back into the room. I could still hear him ripping through paper and moving things around in his bedroom. I was just starting to stand up when Joel came rushing back into the living room with something that looked like a mannequin head under his arm. For a brief second, my twisted mind and blurry eyes toyed with the image of him carrying his Momma's head. I pictured him praying to her head at night surrounded by candles. Those were the kind of thoughts that the night inspired; it was ripe for perversion.

I didn't want to know anymore about Joel. My head was foggy from drink and I began to wonder if I could make the walk back to my apartment. I patted my pockets and felt the comforting clinking of my apartment keys. I thought of Harold— I would have been much safer if I had stayed at home with her. I would have been much better off peering into the world of my Mexican neighbors rather than experiencing the real world of Joel.

"Where are you going?!" Joel demanded when he saw me head for the door. He didn't wait for my answer, "Come and look at the head I made in Mortuary School."

During Mortuary College, we learned throughout the program to sculpt different facial features out of clay. We had to know each feature, its shape and special contours, to learn to recreate mutilated, amputated, or deformed features for viewing. At the beginning of the term, we made noses; and then moved on to ears, eyelids, lips, and finally facial proportions and the lines of the face.

As a final test that we had mastered the Restorative Arts, we were instructed to sculpt an entire head out of wax, based on a photograph of someone of our choice. We were graded on facial measurements, proportions, and aesthetic appeal. It was quite an endeavor, and we were given the entire last semester to complete it.

I recalled how I agonized over picking my subject for sculpture. There were so many deserving faces— old male actors with craggy folds and an abundance of distinctive acquired lines; beautiful smooth-lined women; even my deceased Grandma. The world seemed utterly swarming with fleshy masks, each begging to be the one. All the students in my class poured over photo books, secretly hoping that theirs would be the best, and that it would be displayed in the glass case in the College lobby with the heads sculpted by the best of the best throughout the years. My subject was Frida Kahlo, my Mom's favorite Mexican Artist; although sadly enough, it was less than mediocre, with a mouth that looked suspiciously like a toilet. I threw the head into the dumpster after school let out and my young marriage ended in quiet divorce— both realities that were shed naturally as life moved ahead.

I snapped back into the evening with Joel as he set his sculpted head on the messy dinner table.

Miles rolled his eyes and said with obvious disdain, "Oh, not the head again... Really, Joel."

It was Joel. He had sculpted his own face.

The room seemed to spin as I stared at that strange wax head sitting amidst over-turned glasses and serving platters with scraps of salmon in congealing sauce and asparagus tips on them. I tried hard to be sober as I drew nearer to it. I thought if I didn't look at it carefully that the next day I would wonder of that night had all been a dream. Joel stood proudly with his hands on his hips as Miles got up to make himself another drink. Miles was muttering something under his breath and waxing in the lackadaisical.

I was close to the table now, real close. I had never seen anything like the head Joel had sculpted in his own likeness. The head at once confirmed the degree of Joel's genius and the depth of his sickness.

The shape was perfect, the eyes close set, it even had a pair of thin black metal framed prescription glasses on it that must have been Joel's at one time. The lips were shaped into his familiar scowl and were precise right down to the tiny vertical lines that disappeared into the line of closure, where the red membranes met. The nostrils were flared slightly, giving the whole sculpture the appearance of someone trying to take in a deep breath. (Or someone who was getting ready to scream.) The closed eyelids had lashes that must have been painstakingly placed in a few strands at a time, and the eyebrows had the same precision placement. The shape of the eyebrows matched Joel's stunningly; he had even made the right brow fuller near the bridge of the nose, just like his own.

Joel created a monument to himself.

I stared at it in horror. He must have stared at himself for hours to create such a likeness— such an embarrassment of vanity and splendor.

I traveled back in my mind to a time when I was younger. I was sitting on the floor of my Mom's Art Gallery, watching her arrange paintings as the smoke from her cigarette trailed lazily behind her. "Artists are by definition narcissists, Louise," she told me. "They must consume and ingest and spew forth. They are in constant search for fodder. They must be self-centered. That is what makes them great."

The sound of Joel's high-pitched voice jerked me back into his apartment… and back into the strange and sad perversity of the wax head before me. "I used my own hair; I grew it out all semester to have enough," he said, sitting down in a dinner chair so he could be closer to the head, his glassy green eyes gazing lovingly upon his work.

I backed away from the table, trying to balance myself. "I gotta go home," I mumbled, breaking for the door.

"Wait!" Now it was Miles's voice that called to me. "Louise, wait…"

Miles caught up to me a couple steps outside the apartment door.

I looked at him, but kept my body turned in the direction to leave.

Miles wore a strange look. "I'm dying, Louise." He said quietly. "I have AIDS and I am dying."

I turned to face him. I drank way too much. The salmon and the Tequila were fighting in my stomach. I took in a breath of the cool night air and looked at him helplessly.

"I am going back to Pennsylvania to die. I won't be able to look after Joel anymore."

I looked at the beautiful dark haired Miles. He stood before me with dignity and sadness in his huge eyes. He looked no older than a high school student right then. Miles might soon be covered in black cancer and his own feces and vomit, naked on a table with his purple-tipped tongue lolling to one side— this beautiful boy. I couldn't bear the thought of his beautiful white skin turned to mess.

Suddenly, I understood why I was brought there. Miles wanted me to watch out for Joel. He needed to know that all his obligations would be cared for so that he could go home to die.

I bit my lip and felt my eyes start to sting.

I shook my head. "I don't know if I can help." My pragmatic side even under the influence was doubtful that anyone could properly look after Joel.

Miles shook his head and stared at me hard, "You are the only one. It has to be you. I knew it from the moment he first started talking about you. He kept talking about the new girl with the white sweater. He said he could be himself with you... that you were different, unlike the rest of the Bible beaters around the mortuary."

I looked past Miles through the open door into the apartment and I could just make out the two Joel's, one of flesh and one of wax, locked in a silent stare.

I shook my head. "Nobody can do what you are asking."

Miles smiled a sad smile, one filled with the wisdom of one who knows he was dying, "Then, how about you just tell me that you will, even if you don't mean it. I need to hear it."

I swallowed hard and my nose was starting to run. Messy snot, messy words, messy deaths that had not yet occurred.

On impulse, I stepped forward and I hugged Miles hard. He immediately returned the embrace and I thought I heard him make a strange noise, like a strangled cry. When I pulled back, I saw he was smiling.

"Thank you." He said, confident that my hug was agreement to do his bidding.

But I hadn't agreed. I knew I could barely watch out for myself. For a moment I wished I hadn't gone to Joel's apartment that night, hadn't met the doe-eyed

Miles— hadn't collected another guilty rock in my sack of things I had not done well.

I started walking away, closing one eye so that I could keep myself on the narrow walkway. I heard Miles laugh when I accidentally veered right and walked in the ice-plant in front of Joel's front porch.

"Be safe," Miles called after me. "Call us when you get home so we don't worry."

I didn't turn around. "Okay," I lied, knowing I wouldn't call— another messy lie (another crime against Aaron's watchful God). I wiped my nose on the back of my shirt sleeve, not caring if he saw me. The warm night air hung quiet, like it was watching me— waiting for me to do something.

I made the short walk over to my building and fumbled with my key for a couple minutes before I got the door open.

I made arrangements every day for people who had lost a loved one, yet I fell apart when a living man presented his death to me in person. This was not part of my training and I stumbled over it and failed miserably.

I went in and threw up in the kitchen sink.

CHAPTER 15

On Sunday afternoon, I marched my aching head and upset stomach down to the hair salon and had the stylist cut my hair the way I used to wear it; when things were simpler.

It made me a little sad when I looked in the mirror. I realized that the last time I had sported that little black bob with bangs, things had been a lot different.

I had been different.

Now I felt sort of stretched out. Life just kept running in slow, tireless circles, pushing and pulling— the places I had lived and the people I had met, and the schools I had studied in.

When the stylist was done, she turned my chair around slowly so I could admire her work in the mirror.

A girl with a distinct frown and a pale face stared back at me in the reflection. She looked older and less charming than I remembered. She didn't look like the same shit-kicker that had graduated Mortuary College and left a cheating husband without ever looking back. In fact, she looked fairly tired.

I brushed my hair and applied lipstick in an attempt at significance but I was still there— my round face— my tell-tale eyes.

After I got back to my apartment, my Mom called.

"It's not your fault," she soothed me, blowing her smoke through the mouthpiece, "that the things you see make you hurt. It's not your fault that the little things make you sick. You have always had a sensitive stomach. I remember that you didn't even get through a holiday without throwing up at least once until you were almost nine years old." She laughed at the memory.

I wondered what would become of Joel. I wondered if Martin ever thought about me and felt butterflies. I wondered if Miles was afraid to die. Finally, I wondered if all the things my Mom put into my head were in more ways beneficial or harmful to me; but I suppose it was a never-ending conundrum.

"I remember when you were just a tiny baby in my arms," Mom was saying. "My little sunshine girl... that's what I used to call you."

Sunday evening, Martin and I went to dinner at the local diner. We ate there on most Sunday nights.

We sat across from each other in the familiar vinyl booth, waiting for our food. I kept the events of the night before to myself.

I stared straight ahead.

He stared at the table.

He lit a cigarette. I watched the tip grow crimson red

and begin to dance as he sucked air and smoke into his lungs. Finally, it turned mostly into gray ash with a red glowing center. Tiny bits of ash broke away and played in the invisible air currents, and landed ultimately near the end of the brown veneer table or wafted off over the edge.

Watching Martin play so casually with the world's wanton desire to catch fire and burst into flames was like waiting for God to show up. He looked up and blew a misshapen smoke ring in my direction.

"Hey look, Lou," he said in a relaxed tone. "I made a heart for you."

The lopsided heart broke before it reached me and disappeared into a smoky haze.

I missed my old city and my old friends; and for some reason, I missed my ex-husband. I would have done anything at that moment to just go back home.

My fried chicken and mashed potato platter arrived just in time to quell the storm.

CHAPTER 16

Monday morning, Joel staggered into the employee lounge late. Joel was never late.

Lisa was preparing her instant oatmeal in her coffee cup; Hank was falling asleep in one of the swivel chairs (a common morning ritual); Martin was making coffee; and I was reading everyone's Horoscope out of the daily newspaper.

I didn't look up as Joel entered, and my strangeness over the weekend's events caused me to fidget.

"Martin, you are having a five star day today..." I read.

"Oooooh... Martin..." Lisa said, smiling. "Good for you."

"Lucky me," Martin said, only mildly interested.

I had been reading his Horoscope to him for more than a year now, and he always had the same, mildly interested reaction to it. However, he was the first to complain if I skipped a day. (Routines were what helped the both of us survive.)

"It says that you are supposed to communicate with a

partner whose ideas will give you valuable insight," I continued. "I'm almost sure that they mean me."

Martin rolled his eyes. "You've never had a valuable insight in your life."

I still did not look at Joel, but every cell in my body was alert to his presence, and every second that passed made me more uncomfortable. Out of the corner of my eye, I noticed that he stood in front of the schedule board, with his back to the rest of us. Should I look at him? I wondered. Should I smile? Miles's face popped into my mind and I pushed it away. The whole night at Joel's apartment seemed like a dream. The truth was I didn't know how to be close to Joel. I was realizing that I didn't know how to be close to anybody.

"Good morning, Joel," Lisa said, interrupting our babble.

Martin turned to greet Joel, and I finally looked over at him.

He was plastered. I could see it from across the room. He looked bothered and undone, and his normally perfect hair was ruffled and hung in greasy strings onto his forehead.

Joel turned from the schedule board and headed straight for the coffee without answering them. Lisa stirred her oatmeal, seeming not to notice that Joel had just snubbed her.

Martin shrugged his shoulders at me and pretended to fling a booger at Joel's turned back.

I stifled a giggle.

Martin looked at Hank and asked, "Is Hank asleep?"

Hank's head was all the way back and his mouth was open. His breathing was deep and slow.

"He's been moonlighting again," Lisa said, delicately eating her oatmeal from a plastic spoon. "I swear I don't know why his wife won't get a part-time job. That woman is going to drive him into the grave."

"That's the point isn't, with women? Next time I feel like getting married I am just going to find a woman who hates me and buy her a house instead," Martin said.

I tugged at Martin's suit jacket. "I think I have valuable insight," I whispered, looking offended.

"I know you think you do— but you don't. That's what makes it so funny," he replied, smiling proudly.

I whispered back to him, "I have enough insight not to lock the casket inside the hearse." Now I smiled and he was the one who looked offended.

Martin stuck his tongue out and made a face at me.

"So, how was everyone's weekend?" Lisa asked, sitting down at the table next to us.

"Mine was okay." Martin said. He pointed to the soundly sleeping Hank and said matter-of-factly, "I think we all know how Hank's went."

I grinned, "Maybe we should roll him out into the chapel for viewing."

"I am glad you brought that up," Lisa said, slapping her small hand on the table. "When you guys embalm me, I have a special request... I want you to sheer off some of my hips and give me 'D' cups." She pushed out her tiny chest.

"Well, I don't want anyone embalming me," Martin said, getting up to pour himself another cup of coffee. "Just burn me. Shake and bake, baby!"

"No way," I said, shaking my head. "I am going to embalm you myself... and I will tell you right now that I am NOT going to do a very good job."

Martin grimaced. "Well at least don't let anyone view me for Pete's sake. I'm actually very shy."

Lisa looked genuinely concerned. She never did really understand why Martin and I joked around so much, but then, her job was to answer the phones and type death certificates. At the end of the day, she was always able to leave— and if a family marched in upset with the way a service turned out, she was able to bring them coffee and then run for one of us to meet with them. Her world was much safer.

"But we have to have a viewing for you, Martin," she said worriedly. "There are so many people who would want to come."

"We can just lay him out naked on the front lawn of the mortuary for about a week," I suggested.

Martin looked pained, "The neighborhood cats will love that."

We all laughed, except Joel. I watched him out of the corner of my eye; he was stirring his coffee and regarding us coldly.

Lisa began browsing through the newspapers on the table next to me. As she shuffled through them, she innocently asked, "So Joel, how was your weekend?"

Joel turned from his coffee and flared his nostrils. I lowered my gaze and quickly pretended to be absorbed in the newspaper. "What business is it of yours how my weekend was? I didn't ask you how your weekend was." He put his hands on his hips and stared crossly at her. Nobody besides me really knew if he was joking or not. "You know why I don't ask…?"

Lisa shook her head slowly, unsure of what to say.

"Because I don't really give a crap how your weekend was. And I'll tell you something else; my weekend is my personal private business," Joel put his nose into the air and turned back around to face the schedule board again.

The tension was heavy in the short silence that followed Joel's outburst. I couldn't tell if Lisa was mad or if she was about to cry. I looked at Martin, who raised one eyebrow in question. I silently willed him to say something (because I was afraid too), but he remained quiet and continued reading his sports column.

Hank jerked a little in his sleep and began snoring softly.

"Well anyway," I finally said, my voice ripping through the thick silence, "Lisa, do you want me to read your horoscope?" I smiled at her encouragingly.

But it was Joel who replied, turning on me ferociously. His green eyes were small and mean. His top lip was curled into a greasy sneer. "And another thing…" he snapped loudly, losing his balance in the fast turn-about, causing him to slap his hand down on the counter to steady himself. "I am sick and tired of you reading our horoscopes! Don't you know that horoscopes are considered necromancy by some?! I happen to be a Catholic, but did anyone ever care to ask?!" He looked at his watch and continued on as we all just sat there saying nothing, with Hank snoring in the background. "And how many times has Aaron told us that nobody is supposed to be sitting around after eight o'clock?! And didn't Aaron just give us this entire lecture the other day about eating breakfast at home," he glared at Lisa. "And what about coming to work fully dressed—" he picked up Hank's brown tie that was draped over the back of a chair and not tied around Hank's neck. He flung the tie down on the pink pastel linoleum.

I immediately turned to see if Hank was still sleeping, thinking Joel would be in for a beating if he wasn't. Hank's eyes remained closed.

Martin began gritting his teeth and looking angry.

"You people are stealing, that is essentially what you are doing. You are getting paid to eat your breakfast," he pointed disgustedly at Lisa, whose eyes began to well up with tears. "And you..." he pointed a stubby white finger directly at my face, "are getting paid to practice necromancy. I wonder what our dear old Christian absentee boss would have to say about that."

I thought Martin would jump up to defend my honor, but he just kept sitting there, looking angry.

Hank suddenly started awake with a small snort and began to rub his eyes and look around groggily.

"I wish we could all just do our jobs and then go home again. You people make it so hard." Joel's entire body stiffened as if he was in pain over this fact and he curled his hands into fists that he brought to each side of his head. "Why can't we all just do our jobs and then go home?! You people don't know anything about me anyway!"

Good grief, I thought, has it all come down to this? My cheeks grew hot and my stomach began to rumble. I saw Hank regard Joel with a confused look on his face. Martin, Lisa, and I just looked down.

"You people don't care about shit outside yourselves. My talents are wasted in this crappy place." And with that, Joel walked out in a huff, leaving us in stunned silence.

A couple of seconds later, we heard a loud clatter as he swerved drunkenly into the metal flower stands that lined the back hallway.

Hank looked at me. "Did I miss something?" he asked, looking bewildered and slightly amused at the childish display he had just witnessed.

"Joel just flipped out," Lisa answered, looking hurt. "He is really drunk today. I just asked him how his weekend was... I was just trying to be nice. I always ask everyone how their weekend was. Then he yelled at Louise for reading the horoscopes..."

Hank interrupted her, the amusement draining out of his face. "Joel's drunk?" He asked, looking shocked.

I became instantly annoyed with what I perceived to be Hank's contrived innocence. "Oh, come off it, Hank," I told him with uncharacteristic impatience, "Of course Joel is drunk. He is drunk just like he's been drunk almost every day that I've worked here. At least..." I added, "Every day that Aaron is off."

Hank just sat there looking stunned.

I looked at Martin for support. He wore a serious expression. It made me sad. I had the crazy impulse to lick my finger and stick it in his ear.

"So much pain," Lisa said. Her brow was heavy and her voice dramatic, "Joel carries so much pain inside him."

I looked at her and vaguely wondered how much of that Christian compassion she would muster if she found out that Joel lay down with men. I was still young enough to be fascinated and intolerant of human hypocrisy (even my own). Lisa's first husband turned to a gay lifestyle, something that her fragile ego could never quite bear— and something that her rigid Christian belief system could never tolerate. Her own adult son was gay, and she chose to ignore it. She told me once that if she accepted it, it would encourage him. I looked at her tiny face, puckered in consternation over Joel's dilemma, or perhaps her own.

I finally couldn't take it anymore and I let out a breath and stood up from the table. "I'm calling Aaron," I said, looking at Martin.

Lisa started to say something, but decided better of it and stopped herself.

Martin looked at me in mute agreement. He had a way of communicating with one understated look. A small tic in his facial expression portrayed his discomfort; he drew his lips into a thin horizontal line to suggest anger; a furrow between his brows displayed resolve; and when something in his eyes looked almost hurt— this was the tell-tale sign of his compassion (and compassion was the emotion that seemed to pain him the most). I suppose it may have been compassion for Joel, or us for having to deal with Joel; maybe both. Martin didn't over think his emotions the way I did. He let them come and he let them go— like smoking. Always the smoke.

Aaron didn't answer his phone. I paged him twice and then left a message on his home phone, voicing an urgent need to hear back from him as soon as possible.

I could hear Lisa and Martin explaining Joel's recent transgressions to Hank as I tried to reach Aaron. Hank seemed dumbfounded by all of it. For the first time, I began to look at Hank as less than an artist and an Embalmer extraordinaire. I considered the slight possibility that maybe; just maybe, he was just an aloof and burned out guy in an unhappy marriage. It did seem to me that suddenly there was a shortage of people in the world to look up to. The realization left me soggy.

As I put the phone down, I saw Hank's large frame walking out of the lounge. I thought perhaps he was going to talk to Joel himself; after all, he was the senior man on shift when Aaron was off. Perhaps he would send Joel home for the day and then we could all decompress and try to figure out our next step.

It was about a half an hour before I realized that Hank had left the building. He made the excuse to Lisa he needed to take a rubbing of a headstone at the local cemetery and he was gone for the rest of the day. I began to realize that Hank often left when things got busy or stressful. He was not a hero. He was just a guy who would rather work on his car than work in a mortuary. And so, we were down to Martin, Lisa, and myself; the three newest employees… the three least equipped and least qualified people to diffuse a situation like this.

I began to ask myself what this place did to people…

❊ ❊ ❊

We all retreated into different parts of the mortuary, as if inherently aware that if we were separated then at least two of us would not have a run-in with Joel. Lisa buried herself in paperwork in the front office. Martin went outside and began picking up trash and sweeping the pebbled front walkways. I chose to hide in the preparation room. To retreat was human. Martin seemed most disturbed, and I reckoned that it was because as the last man in the building, the responsibility would fall on him to restrain Joel if things got ugly.

I kept catching myself looking at the phone, waiting for Aaron to call us back. I knew that Aaron would help us. I wondered if we could call the owner. I wondered if anyone had his number. Surely, he would want to know what was going on, wouldn't he?

Joel made individual hells for all of us. We were all locked into Joel's secret alcoholic world. That is what happened when someone hits bottom in front of you. That is what happens when you care. Maybe that feeling is why Martin always looked like he just got punched in the stomach when he felt compassion.

I decided to get a dead woman ready for her viewing the next morning. That would eat up at least a couple of hours and then I could break out of that horrible place and go out to lunch. It was the first time that I sought to flee the small mortuary and protect myself from what went on there. I thought the mortuary would be the beginning of my life, but I looked around and I saw was death happening all around me. What did this place do to people? Why were the three newest hires left holding the bag? Is this what we were all going to become? Where we three the only ones who stayed because we didn't know any better? I thought I might like to strangle Aaron.

I was in the process of using a hypodermic syringe to inject tissue building compound into the dead woman's face when Joel walked in, carrying a stack of books.

I didn't look up at him. I inserted the needle into the standard hidden injection point, behind the tragus of the ear, and injected enough tissue building liquid compound to fill out her emaciated cheek to a robust, healthy fullness.

Joel stood there. "You're getting good."

"Thank you. I learned from the best."

"Yes," he agreed, nodding seriously, "You did." He didn't seem as drunk now. In fact, he looked like he had been crying.

I turned and began flushing out the syringe with tissue builder remover to clean it. *Here we are*, I thought dryly, *apprentice and drunken master.*

"I want to give you these," Joel said, placing the stack of textbooks on the counter next to me.

I looked at the books. They were his books from mortuary school; Embalming: History, Theory & Practice; Advanced Anatomy & Pathology; Funeral Rites & Rituals; Thanatology, etc... Some of them I already had, and some of them I had never seen before.

I looked at him tiredly, "I don't want your books, Joel."

"You have to take them," he said, looking worn and defeated. "I want you to have them. You will put them to best use... more than the rest of these assholes."

"Just go away, Joel," I finally said, which shocked him. "I don't feel like talking to you right now." I wondered where Martin was, and why he didn't come in to save me from this growing menace.

I saw him stiffen. "You'll miss me when I'm gone,"
he retorted, growing mean again. "This place isn't shit
without me. This place's reputation is built on my
bodies! All because of me..." his voice got louder and
he slapped his chest angrily as he spoke. "If you got a
difficult case, you wouldn't know where to begin! You
can't even wax a decent pair of lips! You don't have the
gift. Martin might, but not you. You may as well hear it
from someone who knows..."

I closed my eyes and his words trailed off. I thought
of a million ways to tell him to go screw himself, but as
always when I was most hurt, I found no voice. I could
hear a ringing in my ears. I remembered so long ago
walking in to find another woman in my bed with my
then husband; my ears had started ringing and I couldn't
hear her trying to explain herself. I thought that maybe
my ears knew when to make their own noise. Her words
did not matter. Joel's words did not matter.

When I opened my eyes, I knew the tragedy that was
Joel— cut right in half by the only thing he prided
himself in, a victim of his own art. Martin and I had
spent countless hours studying Joel's technique and it
was our turn now. We didn't need Joel anymore and he
knew it. He wanted me to beg him to stay, to say that we
would be lost without him, but it wasn't true. We both
knew it. He hated me then. I saw it in his angry green
eyes. He had poured himself over me and got angry and
insecure that I had absorbed. I was better than Martin. I
was not better than Joel— but I might be someday.
What that must have done to him...

Joel's face contorted as if he was going to start yelling again, but to my surprise, he slumped over and began sobbing.

"I don't know what you want from me, Joel," I told him with as much kindness as I could muster after the horrible things he had just said to me. "I don't know what to be to you."

"Loulou," he choked out a strangled cry, "My Mother is sick. She might be dying. She wants me to come back home." He covered his face with his hands. "I have to go to her... Miles says I shouldn't go. He doesn't understand. I have to go."

My emotions surged when he said Miles' name. I looked at Joel hopelessly, feeling lost on his emotional roller coaster.

"Miles always hated my Mother. He will never understand." Joel swallowed hard and removed his glasses. His eyes looked small and red and lost. His face contorted.

My God, did they even have a word for the look on his face?

I looked down again. I never had anything good to say, I thought bitterly. Aaron would have brilliant yet stern words of consolation. Aaron would know the perfect time and manner to tell Joel to leave the building. Maybe Joel was right. Maybe I didn't have the gift. Maybe I was forcing an unnatural path. I took off my gloves and lay them down on the counter.

Joel immediately stepped forward and set a neatly typed letter on the counter next to my discarded gloves. "Here is a copy of my resignation letter. I would appreciate it if you see that it gets to Aaron." He wiped his eyes with the back of his hand and put his glasses back on. Then he bowed slightly toward me. "It was an honor to work with you."

He turned and walked out of the preparation room and then out of the mortuary just a couple of moments after that, with his framed Embalming License under his arm. Joel's brilliant career in the funeral profession was over.

Joel's career dropped, sparked, and died.

I stood next to the dead woman on the table and watched him leave on the security monitor in the preparation room. Only after I watched Joel's sporty convertible drive out of the parking lot did I turn and pick out a pale pink nail polish from the cabinet. I held it up to the dress hanging on the cabinet to make sure the color was right and began carefully painting the dead woman's fingernails the way Joel had taught me. The ringing in my ears had died down to a faint hum.

Aaron never did call us back that day. Towards the end of the day, I could hear Aaron's pager beeping from inside his locker. I opened his locker and turned the pager off. It made me think that maybe Aaron was smarter than the rest of us. He knew when to be unreachable. Aaron had been in the profession long enough to see more than one Joel pass through its doors, and more than one well-intentioned and wide-eyed recent college graduate. Maybe that was why the owner was unreachable and the manager left his pager in his locker. The mortuary assembled a strange cast of characters and I felt like I was being sucked into the vortex of misanthropy and resignation.

I tucked Joel's letter into Aaron's message box.

"Should we call Aaron again?" Lisa asked me towards the end of the day.

I shook my head, "Nah. It's over anyway."

Lisa sighed deeply. "What a day," she said. "I don't even know what happened."

"Me neither," Martin added.

I'm just trying to be a mortician, I thought helplessly. I wanted to cry. I didn't understand any of it. Where in the hell was Aaron?

CHAPTER 17

I have only hazy Kerouac style memories of the weeks that ensued Joel's departure. Visions of Martin and I locked in a hasty embrace— and then yanking at our belt buckles blindly, too embarrassed at the un-holiness of our union to make much small-talk. It was pseudo-love. No emotion but to stave off another long night of not being touched or needed. *Should he release himself inside of me? Yes, it's ok. I'm on the pill. No, you aren't smashing me. Is this good for you? I can't see the television... David Letterman is on... I think I'll have a cigarette, what will you have? ... a popsicle...*

Morning came and it was like it never happened. I remember it now in patchy images, the nakedness of his body, and the vanillas and cigarettes smell of his skin, the ashy taste of his mouth. No conscience, save a few quick winces as we passed in the mortuary hall the next morning, dressed in our formal business attire, with our new carnal knowledge hindering our usually easy foray of banter.

It happened several times over the next few weeks—
those late night, three minute grope sessions that ended
with him in a quivering heap on top of me as I watched
David Letterman on the tube over his shoulder. I was
young, and had little sexual conscience. I believed for a
moment that I might be in love. Dreams of funeral
directing became transparent in the hustle of a fast and
empty union.

But now awkwardness replaced comradery and
people continued to die. Working late in the preparation
room was now less about the bodies than about the huge
ghost of would we get naked tonight looming over us.

It's funny, the things that seem to matter at the time-
the love affairs that could have been forever; the nights
that we felt like we would never forget. More and more
that I am older I have an overabundance of these
memories— so many that I lose track. When we are
young, everything means everything, and pain
accompanies time like a second skin. I forgot why I
became a mortician. Nothing seemed to matter except
not being alone and afraid anymore. I was losing track
of my goal. Maybe the dead people were finally getting
to me.

The Martin I knew during the day was a different
creature from the one I knew at night, and he did a
horrible job of melding them into one. I suppose that is
why even now all these years later, I remember only with
shadowed snapshots and fractured body parts, with
David Letterman's voice in the background.

Aaron walked around looking concerned. He
apologized to us for not calling us back the day when
Joel quit, but he didn't explain his avoidance; a point that

made me wrinkle my brow and wonder why. He didn't admit to knowing of Joel's declining alcoholic condition, and he didn't admit to not knowing. Aaron, my elusive and mysterious supervising Embalmer, was completely and maddeningly unreadable.

Aaron kept staring at Martin and I with his grey steely eyes, watching like he knew about our midnight three minute romps, or maybe he was just innocently staring— whatever his gaze meant in that vast mind of his made my cheeks grow hot and I found myself avoiding him. Martin was much more composed under Aaron's possible scrutiny and merely went about his business like a man without a care in the world, a fact which only made me feel more alone than I had before we started sleeping together.

Blood pulsed thick and dark through my tangled vasculature, forcing me to experience everything that life had to offer. If the blood didn't move, then all hope was lost, I thought as I mindlessly embalmed and dressed dead human bodies.

One more family— one more service— one more night on the couch after Martin began his unearthly snoring— one more day working together and pretending it never happened— one more walk past Joel's empty locker...

"You have it easy," I murmured to a dead old woman on the table. Her eyes stayed closed. I looked at the lines on her face as I massaged embalming fluid into her emaciated tissues; carefully, because her skin was as thin and translucent as paper. How do so many people make it through this life? I looked at her misshapen knuckles, large and deformed by arthritis, her sunken cheeks, her skin mottled with age and over-ripeness. Over the steady hums and clicks of the embalming machine, I thought I could hear David Letterman delivering his monologue. The ethereal blood that pulsed languidly through the mortuary slowed and snagged, and mine clotted with it. It seemed that death and loss permeated the walls, even as I let Martin have his three minutes of glory that night just so I could feel someone touching me. I just let him. Just to feel warm for a moment.

Life at the mortuary was slowly becoming unbearable.

I thought sometimes I could hear the dead people falling at night outside my window.

They fell softly
as if they knew they did not matter.

They continued to fall until I came to the window, and in trying to catch them, fell myself.

But I fell softly—
dreamers always would.

CHAPTER 18

I arranged a funeral for a little girl who was stabbed to death in her own bedroom; followed by another arrangement for a teenager who died after a skateboarding accident.

Our schedule board was filled up that morning, and Aaron assigned us two cases each. Little did I know that I had been assigned two cases that would stay with me in nightmares and depression for years.

They were tough arrangements, with both families destroyed and ill-functioning— difficult even, requiring my full attention and involvement. They were both going to be big funerals, with media and crowds necessitating a great deal of planning and organization. Public times- private family times- limousines- pallbearers- obituaries- motor escorts- multiple register book stations so the crowds would not clog in the church lobbies- organists- flowers... so many things to discuss with families who could barely speak.

Will that be Visa or MasterCard? Oh yes, we will take a personal check...let me just write you out a receipt

and you can be on your way back to your empty houses
with their little empty beds where children should have
been sleeping peacefully, dreaming of the things that
children dream about. Can I get you some juice... a
tissue? Please don't think about the fact that your loved
one is oozing and sagging and bleeding over our tables
in the back... forget that we end up so messy. Come back
in your fancy clothes and I will dress your dead in fancy
clothes and spray away all the smells and we can
pretend that the maggots will never come. Can I walk
you to your car and stare at you sadly as you drive away,
assuring you by my confident posture that you are in
good hands...? (You were right about me standing up
straight, Aaron— I can tell it makes them trust me...)
Can I run away screaming from this place instead of
driving to the Medical Examiner to pick up your little
angels that lay in pools of their own blood inside of little
white body bags?

Martin embalmed the teenage boy and I embalmed
the stabbed girl late that night, after files were sorted
through and caskets were ordered. Pretty soon, the
familiar smell of formaldehyde and other embalming
chemicals filled the room and the snaps, clicks, and
whirls of our embalming and feature setting equipment
in the background as we worked on different tables
began its strange symphony. Bodies occupied every
table and the refrigerator was full. We could have
worked all night and never caught up. I began to wonder
why Aaron and Hank always got to leave on time, and
other dark thoughts as I carefully detangled the stabbed
girl's thick blonde hair. It occurred to me that the dead
girl was lovely— a little flower about to bloom. It was

impossible not to look at her stab wounds, impossible not to imagine her struggle and her pain.

I sucked in my breath in a stifled little sob, turning self-consciously away from Martin. My eyes filled with tears and I turned slightly to see if Martin noticed.

He didn't.

✵ ✵ ✵

The next day I told Aaron that I did not want to see any families.

"I have too much paperwork to finish up on my cases from yesterday," I reasoned pleasantly, secretly close to exhaustion, but still too proud to admit it. I was a woman in a man's profession, and I would be damned if they would make me cry uncle.

"I understand," Aaron stared at me for a moment with a look that told me he saw right through my bravado. Only after I folded under his gaze did he turn to Martin. "Martin, I wonder if you wouldn't mind taking the nine' o'clock family."

Martin didn't look up from his newspaper and coffee, simply holding up his hand for the file, in which Lisa promptly deposited the manila folder for the arrangement.

I sighed inwardly. Hank trudged off for the bathroom to do his morning business. I went to my shared desk and began going painstakingly through my funeral arrangements, checking and re-checking everything, nervous at the thought of letting any detail slip by me. My stomach was in knots. My forehead felt greasy. One of my cemeteries had still not confirmed and I was anxiously awaiting a price for one of my obituaries. My knees ached from standing most of last night on the hard terrazzo floor in the preparation room.

Martin entered the office and stared at me lovingly. I immediately furrowed my brow.

"What do you want?" I asked pointedly.

"I need you to see the nine' o'clock family for me," he said in what he thought was his cutest voice. Then he added, "Please." He held the file in his hand like he was praying.

I shook my head. "I can't. I have too much to do for these other cases," I lied.

"Please Lou. I need you to do this so I can see this other family who just walked in. I have worked with this family twice before," he kneeled down on one knee to plead his case. "They asked for me, but out of respect, I wanted to check with you first." He nodded, looking pleased with himself.

"Aaron just told you to see that family," I complained, leaning my head down on the desk.

Martin raised his eyebrows. "Well... now I am telling you to see them."

"I don't have time. I'm still waiting for confirmations and I have to call my families about a couple details."

"Lisa can confirm your stuff for you and call your families."

"Maybe I don't want Lisa calling my families," I shot at him, looking up from the desk. "Can't you just tell that other family to come back this afternoon... then you could see both families and everyone is happy?" I suggested, earning a wry smile from him. If a family walked in without making an appointment, we would only turn them away if every room was full. A family who we let walk out might never come back.

"Have Hank see them," I piped up, eliciting an even wryer smile from him. We both knew Hank wasn't going to volunteer for another family when the Apprentices were available. Hank would pull rank and we both knew it.

"We could ask Aaron," I threw out as my last hope, watching the words disappear like smoke from Martin's cigarette.

"Aaron is too busy," Martin sighed, still kneeling before me with his hands together. "Please, Louise."

I looked skyward. "Fine." I relented grouchily.

He looked at me and tilted his head. "Well, you don't have to be all grumpy."

"Just give me the file," I told him, grabbing it from him. I wasn't in a joking mood.

He scampered away happily, singing out of tune as he went through the doorway, *"Oh, Louise is my friend, oh, Louise is my friend..."*

"Oh shut up," I mumbled, salty and irritated as I went over the file for the nine o'clock family. I thought I might puke if I had more energy. I took out my makeup bag and began blotting my forehead.

Down to my core, I did not want one more tragedy on my plate. I did not think I could stand one more arrangement. I staged my own small rebellion by choosing my darkest red lipstick. Even as I applied my power shade called *diva*, I wondered how much more I could take.

Aaron entered the office and I waited for his usual frown at my vibrant lip color. He ignored it for once, looking me over and then sitting down at the far desk with his paperwork.

"You know, Louise," Aaron began thoughtfully, causing me to still in my chair, "God will never give us more than we can handle in a day."

I looked at him like he was from outer space.

"What?" I asked, a bit louder than I intended. I was all out of sorts and for some reason his statement made me defensive and irritable. I pushed my dark red lips out as far as they would go, trying to make him notice.

He didn't answer me.

Just then Lisa's voice came over the intercom. "Louise, your nine o'clock family is here."

I picked up the file and began moving very slowly out of the office, patting my jacket pocket to check for pencils and pens and smoothing my hair back.

Just as I passed by Aaron, he spoke to me without turning around, "God did not bring you here to abandon you."

I held myself back from giving a snotty retort. I felt like screaming and my cheeks grew hot. I began to blink back tears of anger and frustration. I hated Martin and Aaron and the mortuary and all of the people who kept dying. I hated Aaron for knowing that I was upset and I hated Martin for not knowing. (How could he have sex with me and not know me?) I hated Hank for always being in the bathroom and I hated the owner for not caring. I mean, he must not have cared, right? We were a bunch of figures on a quarterly statement for him. We were cash in his pocket. There was no blood on the owner's hands. I looked down at my hands, all chapped and unwomanly, brined by harsh chemicals and never ending hearse-washing. I bet that the owner's hands were as soft and new as a baby's ass... I'll bet he even had them manicured.

With strength I didn't know I had, I walked up front to meet the nine' o'clock family. I hated them already. Little did I know that this chance meeting would end up changing my life.

I entered the arrangement room to see a pleasant looking older couple. They both rose to shake my hand warmly and introduced me to their adult son, Jake. Jake grinned from ear to ear and looked me right in the eye through his small round spectacles and shook my hand hard. He was tall and lanky with freckles and a slicked back dark brown ponytail, goatee and sideburns. He looked like a rocker type, (just the type that I was not interested in). He had an uncanny joyful exuberance about him, even when tears moistened his eyes as he and his mom looked at memorial folders and poems. His intensity immediately offended me and made me retreat a little.

The funeral arrangement was for the Grandma of the family. The tight little clan regaled me throughout with laughing tales of her better days and their recent trip to London. Jake never took his dark brown eyes off of me and by the end of the arrangement I nearly ran out of the room.

I was sure that he would ask me out at some opportune moment on the day of the funeral and I already felt preemptively guilty for having to turn him down.

However, much to my relief (and my surprised ego), the graveside service came and went without a proposition. The tall freckled young man spent most of the service at my side engaging me in some interesting discourse while his family mingled amongst themselves. He was very bright and most amusing (but so totally not my type). In fact, just when we would be laughing and talking and the moment came where he should have inserted a request for a date, he would instead gaze boldly over my face and grin. This drove me nearly mad with anticipation and by the end of the service; I almost couldn't wait to turn him down just for toying with me for so long. The service ended and after a meaningful goodbye and many handshakes, the family and the boy with the ponytail drove off in a caravan to have lunch; while I was left standing there wondering what just happened.

I stiffened and adjusted the collar on my white lace blouse. Well, nothing like getting passed over by a freckled guy in glasses to make you feel like a real loser. I was going to turn him down anyway, but still something about him spending all that time with me and then not asking to see me again took my confidence down a peg or two. (No doubt Aaron's impish God again, mocking what was left of my spider webbed ego.) I stood there waiting for the cemetery to lower and bury the casket with Grandma Bryan in it and I felt humble.

CHAPTER 19

Martin was the one who finally stopped it.

"I just can't do it," Martin told me after embalming late one night. We sat across a scuffed up brown veneer table at the diner. My pancakes and eggs grew cold and looked strange. I knew something was up because he had been quiet for the past couple of days.

"Why?" I asked, closing my eyes. I breathed in slowly, as if I was trying to differentiate the exact moment when we went from being lovers to being nothing. Our course had run, but I felt sad nonetheless.

"I dunno— lots of reasons..."

"Why can't we just enjoy it while it lasts?" I put my fork down. The cold syrup grew thick on my plate and congealed amongst broken egg yolks. The look of it made me a little sick. "You know, we have both only had these long, involved relationships. Why can't we just enjoy each other... no strings?" I sounded like a man. My loneliness was masculine and without conscience.

He stared at me. He felt sorry for me. I could see it on his face.

I straightened in my chair. "I don't need your pity," I announced abruptly.

He smiled a little at the corners. "Girl, you are so much trouble. I don't think in my whole life I've ever met anyone that is as much trouble as you."

I didn't smile back at him.

"I just can't be casual about this," he said, resuming his monotone prepared speech. I felt like I was watching him from somewhere else. My knees ached from embalming all night on the hard floor. My fatigue made me expressionless as he let me down easy. He continued, "Maybe when I was younger I could have done it, but sex means too much now." He was so uncomfortable that he seemed to be squirming in his seat and I wondered how that could be because except for blinking, he hardly moved. His hand went absently to his cigarette pocket and tapped the pack through the fabric of his pocket— an act of unconscious reassurance.

I stared at him from that empty place. My nostrils still had the lingering odor of formaldehyde and dead people. I smelled it when I looked down at my pancakes and gagged a little. Martin didn't seem to notice.

"The only worthwhile thing I have ever done in my whole life was make my kids," he said quietly. "I would never forgive myself if I took that away from you." He took a sip of his coffee and shrugged, "You would end up resenting me, anyway."

"I want to have kids," I said stupidly. I didn't really want kids. I just didn't know what else to say. I could hear my voice shaking, and I couldn't figure out why.

"It would be a tragedy if you didn't have kids," he pointed his fork at me after taking a huge bite. "Strike that— it would be a crime."

I looked at him miserably, trying to figure out how to get out of the restaurant as soon as possible. I looked down at my silverware, crusted and dried with syrup and egg.

"Oh geez, Lou... please don't make this hard... you look so pretty tonight." He added lamely.

"Maybe I better go," I said beginning to slide out of the booth.

He nodded, looking agonized. "We're still friends, right?"

I grabbed my purse and stood up, my aching knees protested to the sudden movement. I nodded without looking at him.

I could hear him say as I practically ran out of that Denny's and into the dark night, "We are going to own a mortuary together..."

I kept going because I didn't want to cry in front of him. I stopped in front of my crappy little car and fumbled through my huge black purse for my keys.

Mothers were for crying in front of.

My thoughts were filled with fury.

I was furious at what this life had done to me

and how excruciating it was to become a woman—

to be born into a world needing other people and then having to realize that other people were

dangerous

and irregular

and painful.

CHAPTER 20

The next day, for the first time since I had worked at the little cream & brown mortuary- I called in sick.

I drove to my Mom's house and immediately lay my head on her lap. I could smell her perfume mingle with the cigarette smoke, the familiar smell of my youth. The fragrance brought me back to my early and simple times when she would come in from the night air, home from one of her evening art history courses at Cal State Fullerton, smelling like fresh cold night, smoke, and Chanel Number 5. She would lean over to kiss me goodnight and say, *"What fun we will have tomorrow, my little sunshine girl."* Tears began to run down my cheeks.

She smoothed my hair. It made me relax and grow sleepy. I no longer wanted to think of owning my own mortuary or becoming the greatest funeral director in the world. I was sick of the dead people. I was sick of the whole business. I no longer wanted to think about anything but lying on my mom's couch with my head on her lap. I pondered the meaning of success and desire.

Was there anything more safe or warm than lying on your mom's lap and getting your hair stroked? Why bother forging out for some empty existence when so few people ever succeeded in being great.

"Well," Mom said after a long while. "I'm proud of Martin."

I raised my head up a little from her lap to stare at her incredulously. "Proud?" I asked, confused and instantly betrayed. My Mom had always had an abstract way of looking at things. I often failed to understand her words the first time around.

"He knew he had nothing to offer you— not stability, not children… not even youth," she said as she continued to stroke my hair.

I lay my head back down and contemplated this new perspective.

Mom sighed. "How hard it must have been for him to give up such a gem."

We were quiet for a bit after she said that.

"All he has to offer you is friendship, and somewhere in his dried up old perverted heart, he knows that… Thank God!" she added. I looked up at her pretty face framed by her golden hair that no brush could tame. She blew smoke down at me. I watched it float from her mouth and nostrils. I breathed in the Chanel laced smoke and remembered vaguely the feeling of being safe.

"I'm proud that he didn't steal your life from you, because he probably could have." She squeezed my hand.

Could he have?

I thought of how quickly I had let him take me, just to have someone near me again. I silently cursed my own weakness.

I lay there for a long time. Later on Mom got up from the couch and baked little Cornish game hens with herbs from her garden for our dinner. She set the table like she was entertaining royalty, (the way she always did) with fresh cut flowers and square white plates and napkins with tiny little brown and gold leaves on them. She lit the candles before we sat down. That was my mom. It was all in the presentation. She was an expert at making life beautiful. She even made me out to be a gem in my sordid first post divorce affair with an aging apprentice embalmer. She turned me into a gem and changed Martin into a man filled with secret honor and self-sacrifice. She made the flesh and blood of banality disappear in a cloud of smoke.

A few years ago, I learned that Mom was horribly abused as a child by her mother. Each day in her young life brought new and terrible agony as she wondered if this would be the day that her mother would kill her or her younger siblings. Each new day of her young life new horrors abounded. Aaron's benevolent God had some explaining to do as far as I was concerned. For what purpose did his God allow such horrors...such messiness?

Learning this information finally allowed me to make some kind of sense out of my Mom. She was fragile like a dreamer, but she survived the worst horror imaginable because she was also one part forged metal. Mom was a maze of soldered steel intricacies and lace chains, each one folding onto the next. She punished the men who came into her life (including my father) as she would like to punish her own father for not rescuing her from her childhood fate. These psychological and primordial forces stamped out Mom in the flesh; and through such similar inevitable fleshy fate and the bodily assistance of her high school sweetheart— I was born onto her.

I remembered when Mom began her inevitable foray into plastic surgery.

She brought it up casually. "Abdominoplasty with liposuction. My doctor says it will make me feel much better. I have never really gotten used to this belly. The doctor says it isn't healthy anyway." She was referring to her slightly bulging middle. She was not used to carrying any extra weight and the plague of getting older drove her towards desperate measures.

I grimaced. "He reckons cutting you open and taking away your retirement funds is a better solution than eating right and exercising?" While I said this to her over the phone, I found myself cradling my own paunch (made soft from too many Big Macs and super-size fries), riddled with self-doubt.

"There is nothing wrong with feeling my best. I need to feel my best. This will make everything so much better because I will feel better."

And there it was. Remove the offending flesh and everything would be fine. When the flesh that remains is tucked tight and has no visible stretch marks or blemishes, the world could fool itself into thinking that all was well. But morticians knew that we were all the same two centimeters deep. Morticians knew that even the tightest bits of flesh turned green and swelled up in defiant oozing messiness when all was said and done, no matter how much formaldehyde we injected.

A million thoughts flashed through my mind as we sat in the pre-op room not more than a month after that phone conversation. What did this say about growing old gracefully? Was sex appeal really the answer to it all? Was my own belly repulsive? Was my belly the reason my ex-husband cheated on me? Would there never be ultimate rest from the drudgery of having to appear a certain way? Was there any real meaning to life? And why in the hell was I the only one in the room worried when my Mom was sitting there patiently content in her backless gown and tiny socks, smiling to herself and putting on lipstick while waiting to be cut in two?

Let me digress momentarily. I swear it has a point....

At the mortuary, everyone who was employed there had their own troubling case. Each of us had a surprisingly low tolerance for some certain kind of demise, when the rest passed by without much ado. For some it was babies, for others it might be motor-cycle accidents, or adolescent deaths. It was the case that for whatever reason went to a quiet place inside and stayed there for a while. For me it has always been the suicides of old men.

Of course suicides came in on a fairly regular basis. Normally they did not bother me, except when it was an old man. I guess I just hoped that when you got to a certain age, you developed some sort of mastery over this life and all its bullshit. Seeing those old men dead on my table, rope impressions standing out on their necks like twisted braids of irony, it was hard to keep my dream of someday finally figuring out what life was all about. Many of these men had fought in wars and raised families, only to decide at the end that it wasn't really worth the effort. What are the rest of us supposed to make of that?

Mom's perfect scar now ran from hip to hip over her mostly-flat belly. It was her shackle of a life being forced upon her from the time she could remember. Her beauty could save her, if only she could save her beauty. It was the only thing she could ever really rely on.

My hope for understanding life went down the drain with the 10 pounds of skin and mesenteric adipose tissue that they excised or sucked out of my Mom's belly that day.

CHAPTER 21

Feeling frustrated and restless one weekend, I decided to make a pilgrimage back to Orange County, the place that I knew as home, in search of what I might be longing for. I met up with a few friends from high school at a rental house in Costa Mesa.

"Dude, what did you say you were doing now?" One of my best male friends since third grade asked, cracking open another bottle of brew. His name was Robert. He still declared himself a boot-stomping skinhead, and had just finished explaining each of one his tattoos in glorious detail to me as we drank beer and shot Tequila straight from the bottle.

"Embalming," I said, enjoying the weirdness of being back where I might well have belonged.

"Ewww... how revolting!" Shrieked one of my girlfriends, shivering. "What on earth made you decide to do that?!" She wrinkled her pretty nose-job at me.

Robert waved a hand at her, "Shut up, bitch!" He offered me a smoke and I shook my head. The Tequila warmed my insides and made me content.

"Seriously," Robert said, leaning into me, "that mortician shit is so cool. Freaking gnarly and shit!" He spit on me as he talked.

"Thanks." I replied, laughing. "What have you been doing?"

"Oh crap, you know," Robert said, taking a long drag off his cigarette. "Nothing much... I was working for a service garage, but I punched the owner in his face after he got up in my business one day."

"You punched your boss?"

Robert nodded and laughed. "Shit-stain got in my face after I had been fighting with my girlfriend all night the night before. I walk in a little late and he decides to say something smart... the next thing I knew I was throwing fists and people were pulling us apart."

We laughed again and I took another swig of the bottle.

"What are you going to do now?"

"I dunno. Probably work for my dad's plumbing business or something. Who cares?" He flicked his butt onto the dirty linoleum.

William came over and sat beside me on the old flowered couch. I had gone to school with William since elementary age. He had been paying a good deal of attention to me that night. "Mmmmm..." William said, leaning into me, "you smell good. You look good, too. We should go out sometime."

I smiled the smile of the drunk.

The whole scene was kind of weird. It was like I went back to being seventeen years old, partying with the same familiar faces; only we weren't as innocent eyed and hopeful anymore. Most of us were fatter, some had lines on their faces that I didn't remember being there before… and William's hairline was beginning to recede.

In the kitchen, several of the gang was wrapping Shane with a roll of plastic food wrap, splitting guts with laughter as he was spun around and around. Shane was out of his mind on acid that night and he smiled and wobbled unsteadily as his arms were bound tightly to his sides in the rolled plastic wrap. Across the barren living room that was scattered with empty beer cans and cigarette butts, I could see a couple of guys throwing darts into an old peg board that was nailed up on wall in the hallway. They moaned and caterwauled every time their game was interrupted when someone walked by to use the bathroom. The stereo blasted out an old Beastie Boys album from back in the day and completed the surreal vibe.

"Well, well, well…" a familiar voice said, out of the noise, "Look what the cat dragged in!" It was Sadie, an old party buddy. She had dark circles under her eyes and held something behind her back.

I stood up and we hugged and looked each other over. "How cute that you still wear your hair the same way…" Sadie cooed.

I touched my bangs self-consciously. "Oh yeah, I just got them cut not too long ago…"

Sadie brought a bottle of Tequila from around her back and smiled. "Care to join me outside?"

"Sure."

We exited the dirty sliding glass door stood in the quiet night air in the overgrown, junk-filled back lot. "I heard you were a big-shot mortician now."

"Well, not exactly a big-shot one," I admitted half-heartedly, "more like a just starting out and still-forced-to-empty-trashes mortician." Many thoughts rolled through my drunken brain. "Actually, if you want to know the truth, I am thinking of leaving the business." I was surprised to hear those words come out of my mouth. I was in my twenties and already felt burned out. Maybe Aaron was right... that religious asshole.

Sadie pulled a marijuana pipe out of her purse and offered it to me. I shook my head no. She lit the black residue in the bowl with a plastic lighter took a long drag. "Well, that sucks about your job. Man, this is good Mary-J. I got it from my brother. You remember Brandon— he always gets the good stuff..."

"Of course I remember Brandon. I had a monster crush on him back in the day. What's he doing now?"

Sadie fished a tissue out of her purse and began wiping her nose; a habit she'd picked up in high school after a little stint with cocaine. She fished through both nostrils until she was satisfied that they were clean and dry. "He's living with my parents now. His wife ran off and left him with three kids. He's reported her as a missing person." She sniffed and began rubbing her nose again. "He is pretty miserable right now."

"Jesus," I said.

"So, you don't like the funeral business anymore, you say?" She asked, after she exhaled. I smelled the old familiar marijuana smell. Part of me knew she didn't really care.

"I don't know," I smiled, shrugging. "I guess I am kind of going through a crisis right now."

"Is it because of seeing all those cadavers?"

"Cadavers are medical specimens. We just call them bodies." I corrected her in a very Aaron–like way that made me cringe when I heard myself. "Anyway, I guess it's just different than I expected it would be." I looked up at the sky. It felt good to be there. I didn't want to think about being a mortician or anything else but being drunk and having a good time.

"Well tonight, my friend, it is me and you and old times. We are going to keep you up late and party until the sun comes up." Sadie hung an arm around me and grinned.

Robert came staggering out of the house and headed for us. "Hey, I been meaning to ask you something…" he said to me.

"What?" I asked.

"Do you ever see any sexy dead ladies?" He asked me excitedly.

I raised my eyebrows and Sadie gave him a playful slap on the shoulder. "Don't ask her stupid shit like that!" She chastised.

"Seriously, though, man… do you?" Robert pressed on. "Man, I bet you see all kinds of big ole fat ladies, too…" he slapped his knee and squealed like a pig.

I felt anger rise immediately up my spine at his flagrant disrespect to the dead people. I looked at him and narrowed my eyes, ready to unleash my wraith.

Before I could unload, I was interrupted by a strange moan. We all turned our heads to see Shane lying on the brown grass, wrapped in plastic wrap with his arms pinned to his sides. We all immediately cracked up and the tension was broken. Shane saw us laughing at him and started cussing. "Somebody come and cut me out of this! I have to take a piss!"

In the wee hours of the morning, Sadie and I lay next to each other on a twin bed in one of the bedrooms. We stayed on top of the worn yellow blanket because Lord knows what was beneath it. Shane was passed out on the floor and William and Robert were playing video games next to him. They set their empty beer bottles on top of the sleeping Shane and laughed each time one fell off.

I was drunk and drowsy. A long night like so many I had spent with these same people long ago.

"I want you to know that I think it's really cool... how well you've done for yourself," Sadie said, adjusting her pillow.

I snickered in response.

"No, really," she continued, turning to look at me. "I mean, I think about you, you got away from here. You went to college and made something out of yourself."

I felt strange laying there looking at her. I couldn't remember us ever talking about anything serious before. "Don't be too impressed," I finally joked, "I spend most of my time washing cars and cleaning toilets."

She gazed up at the ceiling and looked far away. "I think about starting my own business sometimes..."

"Really?" I asked, curious.

"Yeah, like I could hire myself out to take care of people's plants. You know water and polish them up." She looked at me with a small sparkle in her bloodshot eye, "People don't know how to take care of their plants. If I could get a couple big office buildings, I would be set." She lit her pipe and took a long drag off it.

I watched her as she held her breath and finally released a huge cloud of smoke.

"Hey, pass that over here," Robert said, reaching up to the bed.

Sadie handed the pipe and lighter to him and closed her eyes. I thought she would continue telling me about her dreams, but the next thing I heard from her was the softest little snore. The beeping sounds and gunfire noise from the guy's video game filled up the empty space.

For some reason, I got this feeling in my stomach like I didn't belong there.

I bolted up in bed and rubbed my eyes.

The guys were cheering each other on as they sat in front of the television, too caught up in their game to notice as I left the room.

I tore through the house and out the front door without saying a word to anyone, and I then got in my car and sped away from that house. Without really knowing why, I drove to the apartments where I used to live with my dad. I parked in front of the large building with its huge front windows and began to cry. It was four in the morning.

When there were no more tears, I drove all the way back home to San Diego, the Tequila still coursing through my blood. After I dragged myself into my apartment I fell into bed with Harold, who began to purr and knead me with her paws.

"I don't know where I belong," I told the crazy cat, who stared back at me with her wide yellow eyes. I named her after Harold from the movie *Harold & Maude*. It didn't matter that she was a girl... cats didn't make any fuss over such things as names or growing old or dying.

And part of me always loved skinny little Harold in that film. I thought of the way he ate up his beets in defiance of his mother at their fancy dinner party with his perfect quest for meaning and rage at the hypocrisy of wealth and privilege focused into this one potent and barely acceptable act! *You go, Harold*! I thought to myself in an inebriated and exhausted inner voice, *Eat up those beets! Eat for the rest of us who are trapped at the same table in a world of people content with crystal stemware and plastic surgery and trivial dinner conversation, while their messy guts churn beneath polished skin and manicured nails— disgusted by the reality that they might have to do something so banal as take a crap or puke up bad cheese.*

Next door I could hear the comforting THUMP THUMP THUMP of the bass from the Mexican's stereo.

I fell asleep with my sneakers on.

CHAPTER 22

I arrived for work on Monday morning still slightly green around the gills. Aaron and I went on a Catholic Funeral Service at the local Parrish. A Mass of Christian Burial was a very formal, three part service; consisting of a viewing with Rosary on the first night, followed by a Mass in the Church the next morning, and ending up with a procession to the cemetery for a short graveside service would be followed up with the blessing of the grave.

These rituals needed to be done for any self-respecting Catholic. The new trend toward cremation still had not been formally accepted in the church. Services with cremains (or ashes) present were generally discouraged at that time, a matter that would change in the coming years that eventually ended in Memorial Masses with cremains present as the norm. Memorial is the term morticians used when a body was not present. Funeral is reserved for services with a body present.

Times were a-changing. In the next few years it would become apparent to families that they did not need to pay a funeral home to conduct a service for cremains, which they would soon learn they could handle easily without us (it was quite different than dealing with casketed remains.) People were conducting their own services now, on beaches and in homes. Culture and trends threatened the old school funeral director and it was about this time that 'direct service' facilities with low overhead and cut rate cremations and burials came into mainstream view. We also cringed at the arrival of San Diego's first discount urn and casket store. The employees of the mortuary all laughed at the advertisements for such places in the local newspapers, but beneath our bravado, we stirred our morning drinks nervously and secretly wondered if we were destined to become obsolete tradesmen. I reckon we all privately hoped that the absentee owner had some magic up his sleeve that would protect all our futures in the business.

Unease permeated the funeral profession as creative front-runners scrambled to reach out to the public by way of video display inventory and personalized merchandise including casket engraving and changeable corner pieces. Musty casket display rooms were gutted and replaced with reception areas with food preparation facilities. Urn selections grew larger, and more creative, with the advent of keepsake necklaces and ornamental sculpture that held a portion of the cremains. One company even surfaced that would turn your cremains into a real diamond, and another would launch your cremains into space to orbit the earth in eternal rest.

"Soon they won't need us anymore," Hank sulked bitterly whenever he heard of the next big thing. "Embalmers won't exist, or maybe they will just need only one of us per mortuary. You should listen to me— I have been in this business for a long time and I know a thing or two 'bout a thing or two."

I thought of Hank's words as Aaron and I lead the casket feet first down the center aisle of the formal, high-ceilinged church past rows of standing mourners. I stared straight ahead, just like Aaron told me to so long ago. I tried not to notice the sobbing people near the front, keeping my gaze stoic and slightly averted so as not to attract attention away from the family. Delicate smoky tendrils of incense weaved their way slowly up into the air from their pots at the pulpit. I loved the smell.

Aaron and I had our parts memorized and the entry went without a hitch. I stared at the small wooden carvings above each stained glass window that depicted the crucifixion of Jesus; from him carrying his heavy cross to being nailed up upon it. I wondered why this one act seemed so important all these years later. I wondered why this suffering was so important when so many still suffered. I thought of the murdered girl and how scared she must have been the night that her killer crept into her room. The suffering went on and on.

After the pallbearers and family were seated, Aaron and I genuflected simultaneously in front of the altar and exited up the side aisles. The familiar twinge of excitement of perfect execution failed to hit me as we exited the church at the back. It seemed there was no passion left in me for such things.

For about the next forty minutes, our job was simply to stand outside in the crisp morning air and wait.

I leaned against the brick wall that surrounded the church, lost in thought.

"Louise," Aaron said, watching me curiously, "are you all right lately?"

His voice pulled me from my thoughts. I squinted in the bright morning sun. "What do you mean?" I asked. I was not all right about so many things.

He smiled and thought for a few seconds. Aaron always thought before he spoke, a fact that drove me nuts if I was in a hurry. Incidentally, Aaron instinctively knew that I was ALWAYS in a hurry and he also knew it bothered me to no end that I had to stand there out of respect and wait for him to speak. My supervising Embalmer was a naughty sort. "Are you happy?"

"No," I said flatly, checking my watch. "I am not very happy at this time."

"Is there anything I can do?" He asked.

"Not that I can think of. Thanks though." I thought seriously for a moment. "I have been reading a lot of Herman Hesse lately." I added, as if this would explain my recent restlessness.

"Aha," he said softly, and nodded his head in understanding.

He hummed a little bit. Probably some religious tune. He often hummed while he thought. I wrinkled my forehead.

"Do you think that if you and Martin got married, you would still be as good of friends?" he asked, out of the blue.

I grew irritated, but didn't have the energy to react. Aaron was uncanny at times. How such a devout Christian could possess psychic mind powers was beyond me. "Where did you pull that thought out of?" I asked. As far as anyone knew, Martin and I had never been more than friends.

Aaron shrugged, placing his small masculine hands into the pressed pockets of his grey woolen suit. "I was just thinking that if anything ever happened between you two, that it might ruin the friendship."

"Probably," I agreed casually. *Not that it's any of your business, anyway,* I thought testily. I checked my watch again. I became uncomfortably aware that Martin and I were neither lovers nor friends at that point. My temper rose instantly and then slowly ebbed away.

We stood there for a while in silence, my master Embalmer and I.

I watched him out of the corner of my eye, wondering what he knew. What would he say if he knew that Martin and I had lay naked together, holding on for dear life? What would he say if I told him that the reason that I was not happy was because the friendship was probably already ruined? Did he know?

The judgmental bastard!

"Well," Aaron said finally, adding a comforting smile in my general direction. "I'm sure that you two will do the right thing, God willing." He patted my shoulder and walked away humming a little tune, and left me standing there with my back against the church with my psychological mouth hanging open.

Once upon a time, Aaron was married and had three kids. He said that one day God spoke to him and told him to convert from the Church of Latter Day Saints (Mormon) to Christianity. In retaliation, his Mormon wife took his kids and left the state. He was so pure in his conversion and his belief that God had actually spoken to him, that he let her and the kids go.

I thought Aaron was crazy to choose a religion over a lover and his family. I wondered if his God approved of this. As a child of divorce myself, I wondered what kind of God would want a man to break up his family.

I watched his lithe form walking lightly across the brilliant green of the manicured church lawn, humming contentedly while occasionally looking up at the sky and smiling like he was in on some personal joke with his God. He looked like a man without a care in the world.

I realized that I had never held a conviction like Aaron did... one that was so strong it could tear my world apart. Most of my life was still confined by fear and propriety. *God never speaks to me, not even a pretend one...* I thought, growing a bit huffy.

It almost made me envy him.

I decided to make a mental list of my resources. I knew embalming. I knew it in my bones. Sometimes I think I have always embalmed, even before I was born. That is how it fits me. I knew that when I practice my craft, I am closer to something bigger than this life. I knew that for the little baby I injected and washed last month (his death caused by beatings from his own parents) that his only peace in this world had been on my table. Quiet at last. No more punishments for that little one.

I knew Mom, pound for pound, flesh for flesh. I knew the horrors of her childhood; I knew her hopes and her fears. I even knew how she loves, from behind layers of hurts. I knew that what she needs comes first. I knew that she lies if it pleases her. She told only ultimate truths, and was unconcerned with the rest of society's rules of honesty. I knew that she needed me to love her, if for no other reason, than that I always have.

The things I did not know loom overhead like an impossible tower. I did not know why a little baby gets born into a life for two years of beatings and torture while my life was relatively free from tragedy. I did not know why I couldn't feel happy anymore. I did not even know if Aaron wasn't right when he mentioned one day that perhaps my strange and undying love for my Mom indicated some sort of psychological defect in me.

I knew that if you use too strong a formaldehyde index on a jaundice case that the skin would turn from yellow to green.

I knew that fireworks were illegal in most counties.

I knew that the owner of the mortuary stayed away because he was scared (and I knew that I didn't blame him for being scared).

I knew that Martin perfumed the air with cigarettes and vanilla.

I knew that a person will kill themselves by any means necessary when they decide that their life should end.

I knew that hospitals have a birthing floor and a morgue.

I knew that my cat Harold liked it when I came home.

I knew that bodies found in the water usually smell the worst.

I knew that Mom's house was clean and smelled good.

I knew that buckling up or wearing a helmet didn't always save you.

I knew that my ex-husband lied when he said he would love me forever.

I knew that becoming a mortician wasn't exactly what I had expected.

And I knew that flesh was messy.

✻ ✻ ✻

"You got a letter from a family," Lisa said as I came into the office after Aaron and I finished the Catholic service. "It's in your box."

"Ok," I said, genuinely disinterested. I grabbed my messages and the letter and returned to my desk. Hank was sleeping at his desk with his face planted down by his keyboard, snoring softly. Candy wrappers and empty soda cans surrounded him.

I looked at my messages and then opened the letter. It was from the tall thin young man with the ponytail from the family that I had helped the week before. It was handwritten in a silly school-boyish scrawl of someone who was not quite used to writing in cursive. His name was Jake. I remembered his face instantly.

In his letter he said how I interested him and that he would like to call me to talk. I smiled at its simple sweetness. I told myself it meant nothing, not to mention the fact that it would be highly unprofessional to form a personal relationship with a client. Yes, it meant nothing... but then I remembered the way he looked at me— like he was awake and alive, or maybe I was just imagining things.

I folded it back up and put in my desk. Maybe someday I would write back just to be polite.

CHAPTER 23

In contrast to my dwindling social life, by this time in my career, I was starting to grow more confident in my funeral directing capabilities. It was so busy; I didn't have much of a choice.

My caseload was now equal to Hank and Aaron's. I handled most families with finesse, no more of those careless slip-ups that all newcomers make such as walking into the arrangement room and uttering the cursed, *"Good morning."* After which you would inwardly cringe as some hurt and vocal member of the family would charge, *"And just what is so good about the morning your Dad dies?!"*

For as long as I could remember, I wanted to direct funerals. I wanted to be a part of that secret world. I realized that I may have been searching for something. The fact was, I never learned how to get over any loss, big or small, death or otherwise. Life was one huge hole of grief that ever broadened; and each new loss deepened the fissure— my parent's divorce, my divorce, losing Martin, losing my virginity, changing jobs, finishing college... so that I found myself living in a constant state of grief.

I had one particularly vivid memory of my hyper-salivating anatomy teacher, Mr. Stoia— who stood in front of the classroom on a warm afternoon arguing with a female student who was telling him that she had a tendency to get very emotionally attached to the families she saw at the mortuary she was apprenticing for. This student was very proud of the fact that she often cried with the family during the arrangements. She felt it showed people that she truly cared.

Mr. Stoia was not impressed in the least. "You do not show your compassion to a family who walks into your office by crying with them," he said, shaking his head. He looked at us seriously, the passion in his eyes gleaming as he searched our many faces for any sign of understanding. "You show your compassion to a family that is grieving by doing your job in a caring, competent, and professional manner. You show them compassion only by knowing their options and knowing your job. They don't need your tears. They have come to you because in our modern age of institutionalized deaths, the funeral director is a necessary evil. They don't want to meet you... they don't even want to step foot inside your building. Are you people listening to me?!

"You do these things, and you do them without rushing or up-selling. You do these things with dignity and efficiency and respect, and guess what? They WILL remember you— the next time someone dies. They may even thank you; but probably not. If you crave adoration and recognition, then pick another profession! Do you people understand me or should I write the number of the nearest trucking school on the chalkboard?!"

I watched the spittle fly out of his mouth and gather in white clumps in the corners of his lips. He searched the class with his old eyes. No one said a word.

"I never know if I am getting through to any of you," he finally said, and shook his head. Mr. Stoia lastly looked upon the student who started the conversation, who was by that time nearly in tears. He saw this and he patted her small white hand with surprising tenderness. When she gazed up at him he looked at her encouragingly. "Anyway dear-heart," he said very quietly, "you try to care for everyone, and you aren't going to last five years in this business, believe me when I tell you that." He winked at her and continued the lesson.

All the while, back at the mortuary, people continued to die— an old woman in a convalescent home, an elderly man in his sleep next to his slumbering wife who wouldn't notice him until she tried to wake him for breakfast, a woman in her late thirties from cancer, the list went on.

It wasn't fair when people asked me if I got hardened. We all got used to things if we saw them enough. However, that question always seemed to imply that I developed a lack of caring.

My old anatomy teacher had it pegged right, as far as I was concerned. I cared enough to watch people like Joel— tolerating his insanity so I could learn my trade. I cared enough to sit through hours of anatomy, microbiology and thanatochemistry. I cared enough to wash feces from backsides and clean blood and purge from mouths and scrape it out of hair strand by strand (flesh could be so messy). I cared enough to sit in a room with grieving strangers and help them plan funerals.

That was how I honored life… it was all I knew.

I sat thinking about Martin, Aaron, Miles, Mr. Stoia, Hank, Joel, and all of the dead people whose lives I had gotten a glimpse of during my apprenticeship at the little mortuary. To think that all separating us from the dead people was pumping blood gave me new awareness how close we were to being dead; and it also made me think of how close the dead people were to being alive… to confusion, sex, family, suffering, working, and having complicated and messy, fleshy lives. (Such havoc when the blood pumped!)

Whatever particular realization on that day that led me to call the tall young man with the dark brown ponytail and small round glasses; I could never be sure.

Jake was happy that I called and he invited me on a date with him to the San Diego Zoo. His voice sounded very nasally and high, not like other guys. His speech was fast and quick, with hints of intelligent cockiness. My heart was not in it, but he seemed very dear and polite, so I accepted the offer and then hung up the phone. Then I sat there and stared at the phone and chewed on my hair for a long time in stoned silence, wondering what I had done.

My thoughts were finally interrupted by Lisa on the intercom, "Louise, there is a caller asking for funeral prices on embalming and shipping to Texas on line two."

CHAPTER 24

The next afternoon I conducted the graveside for an elderly gentlemen's wife. The couple had been married for fifty-six years; more than twice as long as I had been alive.

Several days earlier, he had walked into the arrangement with her burial garment over his arm— a pink taffeta dress with small white flowers on it. "I know that nobody will see her in it, but I know she would want to look her best," he explained as he handed the dress to me.

The husband chose a simple graveside service with the pastor from their church officiating. The last of his small remaining friends and family attended; they numbered six in all.

The graveside took place on a Wednesday morning, at our local cemetery that was covered in Oak trees. The group invited me into their prayer circle and I hesitantly stepped forward to join hands with them. Aaron snickered behind me as I was forced to hold hands and pray out of respect; he was beside himself with delight at

the thought of me doing anything even remotely
religious or holy. I threw an uncomfortable glance
Aaron's way as soon as the prayer ended and the family
had turned away from us. He nodded and covered his
mouth with his hand to hide his mirth.

The old man walked with painful deliberateness over
to his wife's casket and placed his hand gently on the lid.
His hand was manly, although withered with age and
mottled by black patches (senile ecchymoses) and age
spots, and it had a tremor.

Then he turned and made a slow but determined path
toward me. I took a few steps toward him as he
struggled on the cemetery's slanted hillside.

He raised his thin frame up and put his hands firmly
on my shoulders. It struck me how strong his grip was.

"May I help you back to your car?" I asked in a
trained, pleasant voice.

He waved his hand as if he was waving away my
question like a small gnat. The sudden motion startled
me.

"I am next," he whispered to me in a quiet voice, like
he didn't want the others to know. "I want you to take
care of me and I want the same casket she had."

I looked at the light grey casket still atop the casket
device over the open grave as if I was making a mental
note of it. Honestly I didn't know what to say. This
wasn't in my textbook or in my training notes from
Aaron.

I looked into his rheumy, phlegmatic blue eyes, all
red and swollen and slightly crusty around the edges.

"I want you to take care of me like you did her," he told me again, squeezing my shoulders so hard that I winced; a command more than a request, imploring even.

"Okay," I said. I found myself rubbing my shoulders after he removed his hands.

He walked away without another word. Without thanks.

Why would he thank me? I was a funeral director and I was paid to bury the dead.

Aaron smiled and nodded as I recanted the exchange. He said it wouldn't be the last time that happened to me and then changed the subject to tease me some about how uncomfortable I looked trying to pray in the circle. "What did you pray about?" he asked me curiously, a smirk on his face.

"I prayed that you would go away," I told him, frowning and heavy minded.

Aaron gave me a strange look that I did not understand after my comment. Was it sadness or disgust or something else? What did he hope for me? What did he want me to be when this was all over? I think I disappointed him on a regular basis by my immaturity and failure to understand the weight of all things. I instantly felt like a jerk for fresh mouthing him when he was probably just trying to lighten the day by teasing a little. But then, Aaron was a man of complexity, and I seldom was able to figure out what motivated him. If he was mad at me one moment, he seemed proud of me the next. I always did try so hard to make him proud, but he would have chastised me for that, too. *Make God proud*, he would have said. I sometimes felt like I could never win.

True to his word, that elderly man who grabbed my shoulders so hard at the graveside died a couple of months later. I dressed him in his best suit and stood in the place where we had prayed in that circle over his wife's grave and watched his 20 gauge steel light grey casket with cream colored crepe interior descend into the earth where his dead sweetheart laid waiting.

CHAPTER 25

Aaron walked into work one morning and set his paper sack lunch and Bible down on the lounge table in a determined way that made the rest of look over at him, wondering to what he owed his morning vigor.

He looked at each one of us in turn, taking his usual Aaron time to form his words before he spoke. I turned my gaze back to my newspaper, my ten second patience quota having run out.

"I want you all to know that I will be leaving the mortuary at the end of this year. I'm going back to school."

We all looked at him.

"Why?" Lisa asked, looking unsure.

Martin and I looked on curiously, waiting for his explanation. I folded my newspaper up and set it aside. Hank stood up and left the room. More and more he had become disconnected from the rest of us.

Aaron pretended not to notice Hank's rude departure; Aaron always rose above Hank's passive aggressive rebellion against all things authoritative. Another secret gift that Aaron's charitable God bestowed on him and denied me.

"I think that I may want to teach," Aaron finally said thoughtfully. "I've been in this field for twenty years, almost half my life. I think it's time for a change."

"What will you teach?" I asked.

"Mortuary Science, maybe. Creative Writing... maybe Theology." He smiled, "I haven't really decided yet. I am content to walk through whatever door God opens."

I looked at Aaron as a man for the first time— a man with his own dreams and desires.

"How come you don't want to be our manager anymore?" Lisa asked sadly as she slowly stirred her soupy oatmeal.

Aaron reached over to me and plucked a black cat hair from my jacket, an act he had done many times on many mornings, but on this morning it made me kind of sad. Before that moment I had always been slightly irritated by his constant grooming of me. Now I sensed that the end of something was nearing, and its dawning left me sifting through the memories of Aaron's daily straightening of my wrinkled collar and removal of Harold's fur from my jackets with a bittersweet nostalgia.

"I'll still be your manager for awhile. I am working on some undergraduate classes now."

Martin rose from his chair and embraced Aaron's smaller frame in a slightly cumbersome hug, "Good luck to you, Aaron. We'll hate to see you go."

"I don't understand," Lisa said over their shoulders. "Don't you like being a mortician?"

Aaron smiled and then pursed his lips thoughtfully. "Do I like being mortician?" He mused aloud.

Lisa took a bite of her oatmeal. Martin looked over at me and his stoic gaze actually held a hint of sadness.

"Do I like being a mortician?" Aaron asked himself again, rubbing his chin and taking a seat. "That is a difficult question." He took a deep breath. "I have been blessed to have experienced a career that has allowed me and my family to be very comfortable financially. I leave with no regrets. When I first started, that would have been easy to answer, but now it has become occluded. Funeral service was something I fell into; I did not choose it the way Martin or Louise did. I can tell you that I do not feel the way I used to feel when I sit in with a family. I find myself wondering what tricks they will use to try to get something out of me, or what discount they will attempt to ruse me out of. No, I do not feel the same way about people; this is one certain fact…" He went on and on after this with similar didactic exploration. His brilliantly trained mouth formed its perfectly pronounced words that came out like honey and concealed any anger or authenticity. He did this for us, I realized. If he ever shared the true extent of his anger over what the profession had taken from him he knew that it would only cause us harm— and that is one thing that Aaron would never intentionally do.

The years of sitting with grieving families had taken its toll. He was done.

Sometime later, after the others had left the break room to begin their daily rituals, Aaron stared at me as he stirred his tea.

"I really wish you would stay," I said, feeling confused. Suddenly I wished I had been a more attentive apprentice. I wished I had asked more questions about fluid concentrations and a dozen other things that now I wondered if I could muddle through without him.

"I have enjoyed a long and productive career. I am now ready to move on." He looked thoughtful for a moment and then said, "I have hired a new apprentice."

I nodded. "Okay."

"You'll have your license by the time I leave," Aaron reminded me. "I thought you should know that I have advised the owner as to who I think should take position of Manager when I am gone." He looked at me meaningfully.

My eyes widened. "Wow... Aaron thanks, but I don't know if I..."

He put up one hand, silencing my fragmented objection. "Let me finish," he said authoritatively, "Did I ever tell you that after my wife left me I got fired for falling asleep during a staff meeting?"

"No."

"Well I did. That was my first job at a mortuary. My world was crumbling around me and I was still trying so desperately to be all things to all people. I didn't even know how to tell anyone when I needed a break for myself. I thought if I just worked harder things would get better, but we don't work in that kind of environment, Louise."

I swallowed hard, trying to understand what he was telling me, as always feeling that I failed to understand the deeper layers of Aaron's words. I thought of Aaron walking by Joel, so obviously drunk on the job. I thought of the way he reacted so calmly to Joel's abrupt resignation, never seeming to want (or need) to know the details from the rest of the staff. How many Joel's had he seen come and go in his career?

"What I am telling you is to be careful, Louise," Aaron continued. "Take your vacations and leave your work *at work*."

I suddenly had an image of me walking out of work at night with the dead people sitting upon my shoulders, one after the other, the unsteady chain extending past the clouds.

"I'll try," I said uncertainly.

"Do more than try. Promise me that if you ever find yourself hating to come here, or sitting in front of a family wishing they'd hurry up so you can go to finish the lunch they interrupted you from... promise me that you will get out."

I nodded dumbly, not completely sure that I hadn't already felt that way on more than one occasion. I was younger and more self-aware, surely that would not happen to me! Surely I would be different.

Everything was changing. Everyone was leaving. I hated it. I wished it could be like it was in the beginning, when I was content just to be allowed to drive the hearse or walk through the cemetery after a graveside and look at the markers. I remembered how proud I was when they issued me my first mortuary pager and I stood posing with it clipped to my slacks in front of the hallway mirror with Joel and Martin laughing at me. My first autopsy embalming that I completed all by myself; my first removal at the Medical Examiner's Office; my first arrangement without Aaron sitting beside me watching and taking notes on my performance... all those first joys seemed so long ago.

As much as I feared his critique, as much as I hated his disappointment over one of my sloppy stitches or out of proportion facial restorations—

I began to miss him, even before he had gone.

It was an ancient tradition, Master and Apprentice. He was inviting me into his footsteps, sensing I was ready before I felt it myself.

"You are almost done with your apprenticeship now, Louise. I am proud of what you have become. Having you for my last apprentice was a gift."

I started to choke up and I looked away.

"God has other plans for me now," he said.

"How do you know that? I mean, do you hear him?"

"I know because I feel him. I know because I believe."

"But I don't understand... what is God?" I looked at him with pleading in my eyes. I wanted him to explain much more to me before he left. Suddenly I felt like I a million fears that only he could answer and time was running out faster than I could think.

"Compassion," Aaron replied.

I let out a frustrated breath. "Compassion for whom?"

Aaron's serious blue eyes darted up to mine, "Compassion for the likes of me and you, my dear."

CHAPTER 26

"I can't go. I'm not going."

"You need to go," Mom told me staunchly.

"I have a zit on my chin. I feel really ugly and my stomach hurts. I don't think I am going to go."

"Your stomach always hurts when you are nervous. Slap on some concealer and the war paint and go out with that boy!"

"My heart isn't in it. I am a really bad faker. I just don't feel like going tonight," I rambled on over the telephone.

"You are going if I have to come over there and drag your butt out to his car. You need to go out with this boy and have some fun. Let him take you out and just have some fun! You don't have to marry the guy! Stop crying over Martin and get yourself dressed."

I instantly furrowed my brow. "I am NOT crying over Martin," I countered bitterly. "I happen to hate Martin. I am just thinking about a lot of things right now. I have a lot on my mind. I need time to myself."

"Have you still been reading Herman Hesse?" she asked pointedly.

I looked at my dog-eared and battle weary paperback copy of *Siddhartha* on the floor where I had dropped it the night before when I fell asleep and I lied, "No."

"Louise Hammond! This is your Mother speaking! I want you to get yourself dressed, put on a smile and have a nice night at the zoo! It will do you good to get out of that mortuary for one night!"

She was right. Hank was embalming my case which I had bribed him dearly for. I might as well enjoy my night off seeing as I would be on call now for the next week for Hank. I was slightly resentful that I would have to take night calls for a week just to go out on a Friday night with a guy that I wasn't even interested in.

I sighed. "Jeez… all right. All-right. Let me go and get dressed."

I could feel her victory waves emanating over the phone.

"Stop gloating already."

"Good luck. I love you." She said resolutely, and hung up on me.

❊ ❊ ❊

He arrived right on time, the boy with the brown ponytail.

I found his grin endearing and irritating at the same time. His lightening fast observations and saucy banter kept me from simmering the way I wanted to in the juices of my sour mood, and that was also irritating.

I had to stay on my toes just to keep up verbally, and despite my best efforts not to, I found myself letting go, laughing and talking with the strange boy who said he worked in a print shop although he fancied himself a drummer. My face must have given me away when he announced this and he smiled and looked me in the eye. Even though his misleading grin suggested he might be laid back, strong determination bubbled below the surface and I could see quite clearly that he was a man not to be trifled with.

"I am a drummer… a damn good one," he stated confidently. He saw me make a doubting face and immediately advanced. "What can you do?"

I narrowed my eyes at him defiantly. "I can find all your major arteries and tie them off with string…"

He laughed and I found myself laughing with him. In fact, it was very hard to keep my smile from breaking my face in half. *Only fake and stupid people could be this happy,* I thought to myself. People that hadn't seen stabbed little girls laid out in little white dresses— people who knew nothing of life's tragedy. I tried to keep myself from liking him too much. He was from another world. How could he ever understand me?

At the end of the date, Jake drove me home. He walked me up three flights of stairs to my apartment after we realized that someone had urinated in the apartment elevator, which I explained was a fairly common event.

I began to grow nervous as we approached my door. I knew he would want to come in, especially since he had gone through all the trouble of walking me to my door. I couldn't imagine kissing the strange man-boy.

He wasn't even my type, what with all those freckles and not even a serious career!

It may be about to get ugly, I realized, and I could feel my cheeks burning in anticipation of a confrontation.

Jake walked gracefully beside me, his smile still there as I fumbled for my keys. I could feel his stare.

After I slid my key determinedly into the lock on my front door, I turned to him perhaps too abruptly, more like a drill sergeant instead of the cool, sophisticated woman I wanted to appear. His smile widened and he waited for me to speak.

"You can't come in," I blurted out.

He laughed a little and held out his hand. His hand had freckles, too. I also noticed his fingers were long and tapered; they looked strong and did not shake the way mine always did.

I looked at him doubtfully.

"Thank you for a wonderful night," he said, offering his hand again. His brown eyes barreled into mine and I felt stripped.

I reached out and shook his hand. His shake was strong, almost bordering on uncomfortable.

I thought he might try to lean in to kiss me, (to which I would have turned him down, of course!) but instead he tilted his head, smiled, and took his leave. I watched him disappear down the long corridor back to the staircase and I wondered what had just happened.

I wondered what made the boy with the brown ponytail so cocky. He drove a beat-up used car and worked in a print shop. He asked out a mortician— and that also made me think he might be a little cuckoo. Still, he had kept me not only engaged in amazing conversation the entire night, but had me struggling to keep pace. He laughed so loudly that people nearby would smile and shake their heads. I laughed at his observations not out of pity, but because he was truly funny.

In fact, I couldn't remember the last time I had smiled or laughed so much. He had a certain John Cusack brand of charm, with his quick talk and his tendency to be earnest and present in the moment. He was similar in features too, and while not definitively masculine or strong; he was attractive and endearing in a boyish way. I was sure I didn't like him.

❅ ❅ ❅

Later on, my mother chastised me for my frigidity.

"Why didn't you just let him kiss you?!" She demanded.

"I am not even sure he wanted to," I said, truthfully.

"I could spank you, Louise! You make the guy walk up three flights of stairs and you don't even invite him in! How could you be so insensitive?"

"He just isn't for me," I said unconvincingly. "He's got all these freckles... and he just seems so..." (*happy*, I wanted to say, he is one of those freaky *happy-go-lucky* people. How on earth could I ever relate? What would one of those happy people ever see in me?) "...so... young."

"I thought you said he was older than you."

"He is... but only by a few years."

My mother sighed and I could tell she was ready to give up. Better for her anyway, I thought. "Well, I guess we won't have to worry about him calling and bugging you anymore. You certainly took care of that."

I wonder, I thought, stroking Harold's soft fur as she lay beside me. I remembered the word ephelis, which was the anatomical term for freckle. I thought of Martin and what he might have been doing at that moment. I wondered if he would be jealous if he knew I had gone out with someone else. I wondered if it would make him change his mind about us. I wondered if my ex-husband, who now seemed a lifetime away, ever thought about me.

Mixing dead people and live people was a tricky endeavor— on one hand, you are constantly reminded to live life to the fullest— on the other hand, you are forced to keep living life one plodding day at a time… eating, pissing, showering, brushing teeth, buying maxi pads… busy yourself with the mundane and the idle, for just a speck of grace now and again. Mom said I was an old soul. I think I was just depressed.

A slight pang of regret passed through my belly and for a moment I wished I had invited him in. Maybe at least I could have given him a kiss on the cheek or something. I shrugged it off and raised my eyes to Aaron's God skeptically. *It's in your hands now,* I thought, willing my eyes past the dingy popcorn ceiling and up to the dark sky above. Maybe Aaron's God was sleeping that late at night. Maybe he wasn't up there at all…

I looked up again while I pondered over Jake's many freckles. What was the plural form of ephelis?

Maybe.

✦ ✦ ✦

Much to my Mother's happy surprise, Jake did call me the next day. He asked me to dinner. I scratched my head and mused in silence. What a strange boy he was, this pony-tailed person.

His vigorous pursuit of me was bound to end unfulfilled. Still, I was curious. I wanted to see what he might do next, this lively fellow— this boy who laughed too loud and looked you straight in the eye. He seemed infinitely too big for his britches. The idea that he was so alive compelled me to venture on. I was drawn to the light at the center, the one he hadn't shown me all of yet.

Maybe just a little bit closer, I thought, I just wanted to see it once, and then I could withdraw. It wouldn't be leading him on, just to get a bit closer. He must have known that I was not open to him, right? After all, he wasn't for me.

Those freckles, for one thing…

CHAPTER 27

The new apprentice embalmer's name was Troy. He left a high paying executive position from some important-sounding corporation to pursue his dream of becoming an Embalmer. He hadn't been to school yet, opting to serve his apprenticeship first.

He flew into our drab world with an explosion of colors and activity. The multi-colored stained glass strained at their ancient hinges as he burst through the door on that first morning and announced his arrival in a huge baritone voice.

Lisa, Martin, and I peered cautiously around the corner as Aaron greeted him, eager to see the new guy. I was eating dry Cheerios from a plastic baggie, Martin sipped black coffee, and Lisa stirred her watery instant oatmeal with varying degrees of expectation. Only Hank remained seated when Aaron finally brought Troy into the employee lounge.

Troy towered over Aaron by at least a foot. He looked like he might even be taller than Martin and Hank. He had a huge mane of thick brown hair that rose straight up in the front and was professionally cut. He wore a pressed, double-breasted olive green suit with a bright white shirt and a beautifully coordinated olive green and black silk tie. I noticed gold cufflinks dangling from his shirt cuffs and an expensive looking gold watch. He wasn't lean like Martin, or thick all over like Hank, but carried his extra girth at his belly that moved when he laughed. He was thirty years old, and wore a huge gold wedding band. His hazel eyes were wild and penetrating and filled with bad boy charm.

Troy greeted each of us warmly in turn, even approaching Hank in the corner and forcing the reluctant loner to engage him. Martin and I exchanged glances when Troy patted Hank's shoulder like they were old friends, not bothering to look down at Hank's expression of bewilderment and distrust. Troy had moved on before he even noticed what a cardinal sin he had committed against our ill-tempered red-haired Embalmer. When he shook my hand, my Cheerios shook in their baggie and my nostrils were filled with his warm, spicy, expensive smelling cologne. He smelled like big business, maybe even a tad on the flashy side.

Troy had busied himself with pouring some coffee and scooping heaping spoonfuls of sugar into it, talking in his huge baritone voice about how happy he was to finally be here, on the road to his dreams. He fit in as well as any of us, I supposed. We were indeed a strange crew of degenerates from all walks of life, bound to funeral service for reasons we could not exactly explain. My own theories about those reasons had wavered over the years, and changed depending on my audience, but how can anyone explain a calling? A calling wasn't supposed to make sense. And for the money (or lack thereof), it sure as hell didn't make sense.

Lisa was taken instantly by Troy's big world charm and sat beside him asking him all sorts of questions. She giggled after each answer like it was the funniest statement she had ever heard. Within minutes, Troy had us all in tears (even Hank) with his ad-libbed impersonation of a drunken funeral director, an alter ego that could have only been pulled off with full commitment to the character, and Troy was committed... in fact, I think he may have been literally committed.

We all tried to keep our laughter to a reserved pitch (after all, we were in a mortuary) as Troy swayed his huge frame from side to side while holding his imaginary bottle of spirits close to his chest, instantly converting his statuesque business-man posture to that of a hunched over, slurring, drunken miscreant who was still trying to function in his professional capacity.

"And now losers (hic), I mean folks..." he muttered, trying to hold onto his pencil and his imaginary booze, his gaze straying off on nothing in particular as he attempted to stop himself from swaying, "I am Troy your duneral firector... and I jus' have ta know if ya wanna a bremation or a curial.... I mean a cremation or a burial... or (hic), ya know wad I mean... oh shit..."

I saw Aaron cringe out of the corner of my eye when Troy said that profanity, but Troy seemed completely unaware of his lack of propriety. I raised one eyebrow at Martin, who nodded at me with a wry smile.

I guess it was fair to say that I liked Troy right away. It was like a tornado had blown in— Troy the tornado. He was irreverent and committed at the same time... a combination that didn't make any sense, but one look in his eyes and you knew that Troy would take care of our families. He was rather like a bull in a china shop in those early days, with testosterone enough for ten men. He was recently married and had just had his first child. He loved to make people laugh and talked openly about his prior addiction to drugs and porn.

The way he talked intrigued me. I had never met anybody so open before— so unashamed. I was ashamed of almost everything, but Troy the tornado just opened his mouth and let his most glorious and most defiling moments run out and swirl together like some magnificent eddy— as if there was no difference; no ego to interrupt or contain them. No fear of judgment, no stopping to make sure that everyone else approved— just an unabashed talent for life and a compelling need to drive the cart forward. I wanted to warn him to be careful, to watch his cussing in front of Aaron and not to touch Hank, but how could I inhibit this work of art in the flesh? Who was I to stifle this force of nature? It wouldn't have done any good anyway. Better to watch… and learn.

Things were definitely going to be different around here, I thought. I could feel Aaron's God looking down on us like organisms in a Petri dish. Add a pinch of Troy to a stagnant situation, stir, and incubate.

CHAPTER 28

Martin's father died that Monday.

He booked a ticket back to his hometown in Oregon for the next day. He spent the next hour complaining about the price of that ticket. I tuned him out and concentrated on my case. Our relationship after our 'breakup' night at Denny's had been confusing and strained. I dealt with the unspoken tension mainly by ignoring him— or at least pretending to.

"I might just stay there, too." Martin said casually in the preparation room.

I stopped the embalming machine on my case so I could hear him better. "What?" My heartbeat sped up a little.

"I said that I might just stay in Oregon. Haven't made up my mind yet." He didn't turn around from the body he was cosmetizing, which kept his back to me.

My eyes widened. "Really? You might be leaving forever?"

"Maybe." He shrugged. "I don't know, LouLou. Since I left wife number two, there isn't much for me here. My family is all in Oregon, including my son, Vic. My first ex-wife has been crying to me lately that he has been messing up in school. He is going to be sixteen soon. He needs me around."

"What about your daughter though? Ellie is only six years old! You would pick up and leave her while she is still a little girl? Don't you ever learn?!" I sounded exasperated. My cheeks grew hot.

He shrugged again, but he was beginning to show signs of frustration from my comment. His back stiffened slightly as he leaned over the body with a tiny lip brush. "It's either one kid or the other... I'm always screwing up someone's life, so what does it really matter?!" He said hotly, waving the tiny brush in my general direction. "I can barely afford to eat between child support and alimony. I rent a tiny room in a crappy house— I can't even smoke inside for shit's sake! Vic's mom keeps calling me and crying about him threatening to blow up the school and whatever. The ex keeps asking for more money. At this rate I will never be able to afford to go to mortuary school."

"Well that's a good thing because you are too dumb to pass the State Boards anyway," I snipped. It felt good to be mean to him. Too good. I felt my fury spinning up and outward.

"Ha ha, that's *soooo* funny," he said snottily. "If I go back to Oregon now, at least I know that I can make enough money logging to support everyone."

"But what about embalming? I thought that you wanted to get licensed. I thought that this was your dream."

"I do want to get licensed. I still do. I will get it one day. Right now, I just want to make things easier."

I finally exploded. Whether it was rage at his rejection of me or the fact that he was an idiot who I falsely idealized, I did not know. "But maybe it isn't meant to be easy!" I raised my voice at him, which seemed to surprise both of us. He finally turned to face me and I continued. "You always just run away when anything gets tough. You left your son when he was a child to start a new life after you screwed his all up... and now you are going to do the same thing to your daughter... and that does not even begin to account for the women who loved you! Maybe if you stayed in one place for any length of time, you would have had time to invest in a career that could pay for all of your mistakes."

Anger flared in his eyes. We had gone to a place that we had never gone before, and it was too late to run back now. I suddenly wanted to tell him everything I knew about him... his depression, his failures, his weaknesses.

"You are too young to understand anything," he spat at me hatefully. *(Was that really hatred in his eyes?)* "If you had any inkling as to what in the hell you were talking about, you would really feel like an idiot right about now!" His voice was shaking. "You come in like you know everything because you had a divorce, when you don't know shit about life! Grow up!" When he turned back to his body, I noticed his neck had grown bright red and a vein stood out noticeably.

I pushed on, too emotionally raw from his recent rejection to control my own emotions. "At least I don't manipulate people. I don't inspire fear in everyone who loves me by threatening to leave at any given moment," I said, causing him to turn and level a steady grey gaze upon me, like he was warning me not to continue. "How can you ever expect anyone to love you? How can you expect to ever have any kind of a life when you are constantly starting over?!"

His nostrils flared, "I never asked anyone to love me... least of all you! You don't know shit about life yet. I have paid for all of my mistakes. I have ALWAYS held up my end of the bargain..." he banged a fist angrily on an embalming table, causing a loud, hollow THUNK sound on the cold steel. "Let's get this straight right here and now, sister... YOU will never be allowed to run my life. Welcome to the real world. You will get jaded one day, mark my words."

"I will never become what you are. I know plenty about life. I know better than to give up."

"You know plenty about life, huh?!"

I nodded.

"You still subscribe to MAD Magazine for Pete's sake..."

"I enjoy the political parody!" I shouted angrily.

"You still watch Pippi Longstocking movies..."

"She is the female superhero of modern literature!" I retorted.

"You are such an infant! You think all the little shit you do actually matters?! Following Joel around like he was some kind of embalming Messiah?! Staying late all the time to work for a man who you have never even met?! You think you are scoring points with someone?! You think guys in the profession like Hank will ever treat you like an equal?! Not likely." He scoffed and his eyes grew little and mean. "I have been alive a hell of a

lot longer than you and I can tell you that this is the only
thing I know for sure— none of it matters, Lou! None of
it!"

"You're an asshole."

He smiled a mean smile and turned back to his case.
"Just might be."

"I hate you!" I shouted. I stood there with blood
dripping off my gloves onto the grey & pink chunked
terrazzo floor.

Suddenly the preparation room door opened and
Hank slowly sauntered in wiping mustard off his tie and
absently headed in the direction of the bathroom that was
at the end of the room. Martin and I both stared at Hank
in enraged silence.

Something in the silence caused Hank to look up
from his tie and he suddenly noticed the tension. Almost
immediately, Hank raised one eyebrow, and without
saying a word, he turned right around and left, shutting
the prep room door quickly behind him.

Martin continued to stand there and seethe at me,
anger clear in his steely eyes. His perpetual standing
hair in the back looked less like a boyish cowlick now
and more like the enraged headpiece of a giant blonde
cockatoo. Boundaries were not only being crossed
during our exchange, but blown into the nether regions.
Rejection fueled my venom. I wanted to lay him down
on an embalming table and pull up one of his crusty
arteries and snap it with my forceps. I was sure that his
arteries with be crunchy and atherosclerotic from his
steady diet of Velveeta cheese rolled inside of salami
slices. Martin was ugly inside and out.

Martin began jerking off his white lab coat. "I don't have to explain anything to you," he tossed the coat uncharacteristically onto the floor and slammed the preparation room door behind him as he huffed out. The whole mortuary must have heard our exchange, but nobody made a sound.

His exit was so dramatically staged that it almost made me giggle, and then, immediately afterward I felt like crying. I stood there with my half-embalmed case and my bloody gloves and no way to stop now. I composed myself for a minute and then resumed my injection.

After I calmed down a little, I decided that I couldn't really blame Martin for wanting to leave; he made a mess of things wherever he went. His two ex-wives (the women who tried to hold onto him the tightest), only had children to show for it, while the elusive man slipped away to somewhere else.

I wondered what Aaron would say that God was trying to teach me in my relationship with Martin. I wondered if maybe God sometimes had no point to make at all. Still, Aaron's repetitive meanderings about God and His infinite plan for our lives made me search for some sort of message that was not being fully revealed to me. Could it be possible?

I guessed that Martin was not meant to be confined; not by a job or a wedding ring, or even a state. Guilt was a strong motivator— but not even guilt over abandoning his children would change his nature. It's difficult sometimes to know how to honor a person. As a mortician, honoring someone was of the highest priority. In my eyes, I gave Martin something that few women had granted him— a clean getaway. I think that God may have approved.

That night I had a dream that I had to embalm Martin. I cut the skin above his sternoclavicular articulation and cigarette smoke began leaking out of the incision. I opened the incision and found no blood— just dried out muscle tissue and smoke-filled arteries. He didn't take the fluid very well and turned out really blotchy. I woke up feeling disappointed in my work.

Martin indicated to Aaron that he would be back in about a week. I was the only one who knew that Martin may have left California for good.

After all that I had learned about Martin, it shouldn't have shocked me that he was able to breathe me in and then let me go, just like everything else. It still hurt, though, to learn that he was one of the dead people. I suppose it is always disheartening to learn that the only one who really thought I was special was mom (and maybe a pot-bellied old anatomy teacher who spit on my face when he talked that I knew once upon a time in what seemed to be a different life).

And maybe, just maybe... God.

Work was extra busy, with Joel gone and now Martin.

It was different, too. It seemed quieter. There was no Martin making wisecracks and cuffing me on the back of the head. I missed his craggy face and his advice on how dark my lipstick should be. I missed his banter, his hard work, and the way his cigarettes and lighter accidentally fell out of his chest pocket several times a day. I missed him at meal times and whenever I had to reach something off a high shelf. I had to ask for Hank's help now, and that was not nearly as much fun.

I missed the way he lingered around. He always had a bit of the Steppenwolf in him—lingering in doorways; the preparation room door, my bedroom door... he never seemed quite sure if he should be coming or going— just as the Steppenwolf lingered on the outskirts of town, attracted by the smells and warmth, but not really a part of this world or that. I wondered if other people missed things as much as I did. The grief was in me; around me and through me— permeating all thoughts.

Martin left and it was only a few days before all of his smoke filled charm was gone. The air just didn't taste as good without him blowing by-products of Marlboro reds into it.

Still, Troy brought his own unique flair to our drab little world. He was a flurry of energy and ideas. He was unbridled and tended to talk over people, making Aaron grimace over his glasses as Troy flooded the families with a dozen ideas at once, wanting so much to be helpful, trying so hard to prove what he knew. Troy inserted his huge countenance into a family's most sensitive moments like an elephant slipping into a

bathtub, but the families responded to him. It wasn't
long (much to Aaron and Hank's chagrin), before people
started asking for Troy by name. "Troy was so
wonderful when our father died," they would say to Lisa
on the phone, "It would be wonderful if we could use
him now for mom."

Troy was not afraid to bear-hug the widows, and
reassuringly back-slap the widowers. He roared with
laughter and radiated warmth that drew people to him.
During his arrangements, it was not uncommon to hear
his laughter and the laughter of his families spill out into
the foyer from the casket room or from the arrangement
office. Laughing! Hank would wrinkle his nose and
remark on Troy's unprofessionalism, but Aaron kept
mostly quiet, watching as Troy quickly learned to be a
huge seller and a remarkable man on services,
conducting them flawlessly with his natural air of
authority and flair for the show.

He changed all the rules— and people loved it.

I made new discoveries on an almost daily basis by
observing Troy. I watched him direct pallbearers in
unison; instructing them to stand shoulder to shoulder
during the graveside instead of having them place the
casket on the lowering device and then return to the
crowd. This new procedure created a human wall of
reverence, allowing the pallbearers to place their
carnation boutonnieres on the casket as their final
blessing at the close. Why didn't I think of that? He was
a stream of ideas and innovation. He sparked in me the
feeling I had when I had first entered the mortuary
doors... like the world could be made better by new

energy and bold epiphanies. Troy brought hope with
him (and just in time.)

Of course Troy did make his share of first-timer
mistakes. He buried a crucifix with the casket on a
Catholic graveside instead of offering it to the family.
He let a family open the casket for a final inspection of
the deceased at the local cemetery, a big no-no that
caused the head of the cemetery crew to yell and shout at
Troy as family members converged emotionally upon the
wobbly casket device placed over the grave. After the
casket was lowered and the family was gone, I watched
in the distance as Troy managed to charm the ill-
tempered, leathery-faced, tobacco-chewing cemetery
supervisor named Max. I shook my head in disbelief
when I saw Troy wrap his big arm around Max's
shoulder and their laughter began to echo up through the
granite headstones and over the cemetery hills.

We watched as Troy tore down the image of the
quiet, almost invisible funeral director. Hank grew more
distant, his morning bathroom breaks extended in time
and then increased in number and frequency until the
better part of every hour was spent in there. Aaron
appeared not to be aware or alarmed by Hank's growing
withdrawal and the rest of us dared not confront him
about it, although I noticed that his sudden evacuation
urges came conspicuously on whenever a new family
walked through our stained glass doors and seemed to
resolve itself by the same mysterious twist of fate after
another one of us was assigned to the case.

We watched as Aaron tried in vain to squelch some
of Troy's bravado and remind him the virtue of listening
rather than talking, of asserting a calm presence rather

than the tornado. Aaron's cryptic guidance and sage advice failed to penetrate Troy's world for the most part, causing Aaron some chagrin, but then funeral and casket sales figures would come in for that month and Aaron's scolding would become less and less until it was finally little more than reminding Troy to refrain from cussing or telling offensive jokes in his presence.

Troy reckoned himself a Christian, and this bothered Aaron as well. (I guessed they were not the same sort of Christians.)

As the sales figures climbed, Aaron's tolerance of Troy climbed with them. Benevolence was a commodity just like all the rest.

CHAPTER 29

I continued to let the freckled pony-tailed boy named Jake come to take me out. Despite my best efforts, I was growing quite comfortable in his company, and it became somewhat of a private joke between us when after each enjoyable excursion, he would escort me to the third floor of my apartment and request to enter. He would laugh good-naturedly when I would deny him access and offer him a handshake. I told him each time that walking me to my door was not necessary, but he insisted, saying that I was a lady, and all ladies should be walked to their doors. And after each denial of passage into my apartment and each handshake, he would call the next day, and ask me out again.

My stomach began to flutter nervously as I waited for him to arrive and I began taking more time in applying my makeup. I began to pass on late-night embalming, and started counting down the minutes for the work-day to end so I could be in his company. For the first time in my short history in funeral service, I did not want to work overtime.

Of course, Jake was an odd boy in a lot of ways. For one thing, he was very loud. His loud talking and laughter often caused people to look over at us when we went to movies and restaurants. Jake of course, seemed not to notice, and when I pointed it out to him, he just grinned and looked at me as if I had said something charming. He was always looking at me like that. I even caught him looking down my blouse one night during dinner when he thought I wasn't paying attention.

There was also the night of the incident at the Mexican Restaurant out by Lake Hodges. We walked over to the lake while we waited for our table. A little boy of no more than six years old was flinging small stones into the lake, clapping his chubby hands and laughing excitedly as they hit the surface.

Jake and I smiled as we watched. The boy picked up another small stone and Jake interrupted him. "You don't want that one," he said, looking around. Jake spotted a boulder sticking up out of the sand that was about the size of a human head. The boy and Jake ran over to it and began using small sticks to dig it out of the ground.

I looked at the boy's worried mother. She still had a polite smile on her face, but her brow wrinkled slightly as her son knelt down in the sand in his dress pants. I grew nervous, thinking that Jake might cause some kind of scene. Even if he managed to get that rock free, it would be near impossible to throw it into the water.

Somehow, Jake heaved that boulder from the earth and with beads of sweat now running down his forehead; he lugged it over to the lake as the boy ran clapping beside him. Jake could not lift the rock very high, in fact it never got past his waist, but when he let it drop into the murky water, it made a huge splash and a great sound like SSWHHEERRPPP as the lake swallowed it up.

My mouth hung slightly open and I saw the young mother run up and grab her clapping and cheering boy who was now splattered in green lake muck from the splash and lead him away, throwing an irritated look towards Jake— who paid absolutely no attention to her.

Afterwards, Jake walked over to me, pulling hair that had come loose during the hefting of the boulder back into his smooth dark ponytail. He wore a proud smile.

I was incensed that he would cause such a ruckus, my hyper-sensitive public image seething with disbelief at his actions.

"You drenched that kid!" I said hotly to Jake. "What in the hell did you think you were doing?!" In my mind I began to assemble all the reasons why what he had just done was completely inappropriate. I sat just waiting to unfurl.

He laughed extra loud, "I'M LIVING, BABY!" he shouted, raising his freckled arms into the air like he had just won a race. People standing further down the shoreline heard his voice and stared at us curiously.

That event stayed on my mind for some time. Jake was infinitely too loud and happy to be a mortician, I thought. I didn't tell anyone from my work about him. He was hardly containable. And all those bright colors he wore! The Fred Flintstone t-shirts, he was so proud to tell how many boxes of Fruity Pebbles he had to eat to earn them. He drew so much attention to himself, and to us. I hated it when people stared. I preferred to be invisible; an observer.

I thought that Jake would be a great man for someone, but definitely not for me. I thought this even after I started to weaken to him and his strange ways. I thought this even after he took me to dinner one night at the restaurant in San Diego that my ex-husband used to take me to on our anniversary. I told him I felt uncomfortable going there and I told him why.

Jake was un-deterred. "But, you said it was your favorite restaurant."

"It is." I told him, "I just have too many old memories there."

"Then let's go make some new memories!" He said determinedly, "Let's go and take this restaurant back!"

That night I ate Linguini with clams in a white cream sauce for dinner and dark chocolate mousse for desert. Jake regaled me with tales from his childhood. I became one of those happy idiots, laughing with him and smiling at nothing in particular. It was one of the best meals I have ever eaten.

During this time, I was always posed and ready to rebuff his advance toward me, but he stayed disconcertingly respectful. He never leaned in for a kiss (to which I would have surely denied him anyway...) which quickly changed my initial feeling of relief to surprise— and ultimately, to downright irritation. Maybe I was reading his signs wrong, but I was beginning to wonder if he would ever make a move. In fact, I began flirting with him shamelessly, for reasons I did not fully understand, trying to seduce him in to making his move so I could finally make it clear to him that I only wanted a friendship.

At work I embalmed dead human remains and met with families and conducted funerals, but things were different somehow. Maybe it was because Martin was in Oregon, or maybe because Tornado Troy had been hired. Maybe it was because I could finally go through a day without thinking about my divorce. Or I guess maybe it could have been partially because of Jake... but probably not.

❊ ❊ ❊

I had a weird dream one night after a date with Jake.

In my dream, I was in a dark and scary place that I did not know. Somewhere off in the distance, over a mass of huddled corpses, I thought I saw one body rise and begin blindly making its way over to where I lay. I was stiff and could not move, and I felt like crying. I could smell smoke in the air and my cheek had saliva on it. "You matter," the corpse whispered, staring at me with cloudy eyes.

I tried to ignore it, and in my dream I donned my autopsy gloves and mask in preparation to do my duty. I looked at the pile of bodies. *It was gonna be a long night*, I thought, *especially if these dead bodies keep trying to get up and walk around.*

The talking corpse continued to speak to me even after I lay him down on the embalming table. He talked right on through my incision and probing and finally the raising of his carotid artery. It was unnerving, but I remained professional in my duty. He talked and mumbled when I inserted the cannula and began injecting fluid into his body. I reckoned he was a pretty nice guy, all in all, despite the strange circumstances.

I remember feeling a bit dismayed when I injected needles and closed his mouth with wire. It was a shame to silence such a likable fellow. He was so cooperative. I embalmed the rest of the bodies in the huge pile and I woke up feeling a little tired.

CHAPTER 30

The religious tension mounted between Aaron and Troy. Morning meetings were often peppered with heated Bible debates, with Lisa always taking Aaron's side. There were diatribes on Tribulations and Revelations and Grace. There was the condemning of Jehovah's Witnesses and Mormons and others that were considered a cult or a sham by both arguers.

Martin had still not come back from Oregon.

Hank went to deliver a casket in Los Angeles early in the morning. He should have been back by mid-afternoon, but he didn't return until 8:00pm. He had the audacity to write it up as overtime on his timecard. Aaron paid him for it without a word. I figured at this point that either Aaron was an idiot, or that Aaron understood on some conscious level that Hank was burning out in his own individual way— just like he did, and just like Joel did.

Hank— Embalmer Extraordinaire; the King of the At-Home Removal; the Man Whom No Foul Smell Ever Conquered...

Hank, who in the end, was just a burnt out, stressed out mortician. I wondered if that would be my fate. Once upon a time I would have never believed it, but seeing my fine comrades go down one after the other was confusing and humbling. The bravado of my earlier days was replaced by a slower, more thoughtful purpose.

Meanwhile, the dead people kept being wheeled in. Christmas was coming— flu season, people in a hurry, people just lining up to punch in their last timecard. I was a madwoman, racing in the van with my cot from place to place, collecting the dead, sliding bodies onto tables, into caskets, scooping cremated remains into fancy pots, sitting with families and filling out vital statistics by hand, leading them into the selection room, watching them wince, waiting as they chose a prayer for their memorial folders, offering tissues as they sobbed over each new page, running out of work each night to go meet with Jake, getting reprimanded by mom for not inviting him in, Sadie calling me from Orange County and asking when I was going to come up and hang out again.

And then one night, moved by something he said, I kissed the pony-tailed boy, and then everything changed.

It all started when we went for ice cream. We ate our brightly colored cones outside the front of my apartment building.

"That is what I love about you," he said.

"What?"

"Look at the way you eat that ice cream cone... with voraciousness! You laugh the same way, with total abandon. Your whole body shakes..."

And then he said something I will never forget.

"…you are so full of life."

"Me?" I coughed, holding my ice cream in mid lick.

"You."

It was the nicest thing anyone had ever said to me.

And then I kissed him. I melted into him. He hugged me tightly and smiled into my mouth. The ice cream fell out of my cone and landed with a soft *splat* on the asphalt. Jake smelled like warm buttered toast. The world shut off.

And then I broke away and turned with a clumsy goodbye and threw my empty cone into some bushes before I literally ran into my building. I left him standing in the parking lot with the bright blue ice cream cone melting in his hand and a smile on his face.

CHAPTER 31

Martin returned to work on a Monday morning. The moment I walked into the mortuary, I knew he was back. I smelled that distinctive mixture of cigarettes and vanilla.

As I put my purse into my locker, I could hear him singing one of his old familiar songs.

"... oh, I love to go swimming with bowl-legged women..." he sang.

Jake's kiss still burned on my lips. My heart beat faster as Martin's voice got closer.

"... and swim between their legs..."

Just then Martin rounded the corner, a cup of coffee in one hand.

"LouLou!" he exclaimed, looking excited.

"Well, welcome back, stranger," I said, smiling.

"Did you miss me?" His low, familiar voice hit me deep.

"Not really."

He slapped me playfully on the back of the head. "Like a hole in the head, right? How has work been?"

"Busy. How was the funeral?"

He paused and looked thoughtful. "It was okay. Mom's holding up better than I thought. She'll be next, though. I don't think she'll last a year."

"Really? I am sorry."

"It's okay though. Really it is." He took a deep breath and then coughed a little. "The old town didn't change very much. Everyone I went to high school with is still pretty much the same. I saw most of my old friends. I don't really fit in any more. It's familiar, but I guess I'm not."

I smiled. He was going to stay in California after all.

He cocked his head and looked at me with one eye narrowed. "Not that I am too fond of California or anything... to me California is like granola..." he paused for a moment (his comedic timing was impeccable), "you take away the fruit and the nuts, and all you've got left are flakes."

I laughed softly and then got quiet. "Hey, I wanted to say that I am sorry, for some of the things I said before you left..."

"Don't worry bout it. You're forgiven."

"I mean it, though..."

"I know you do. I know you do." He looked at me carefully. "You mean everything you say. We're friends, and that doesn't just go away."

"How do you suppose we became friends?" I asked, wrinkling my forehead.

"Hell if I know. You are an awful lot of trouble." He looked at me very seriously. "You look really good. You look like you are glowing," he said, in a manner quite unlike him.

Life would conquer you if you let it. Anxiety, stomachaches, panic, fear… they were the things that occurred when I tried to control life and its tendency to put me into awkward situations.

In that moment, I just gave into things. He didn't have to be mine for me to care about him. The pangs of agony that I always felt in my stomach subsided as my fears began to fade.

Later on that day, I stood dressed in my professional attire at a graveside service. Funerals could be so peaceful. More peaceful, I thought, than anything.

There was this collective silence that was rare among groups of people. You could hear others breathing, sobbing softly— and the sharp resonance of the pastor, repeating godly phrases.

In the near distance, I watched an embarrassed young mother chasing her infant son, who was gleefully plucking trinkets and flowers from the graves as quickly as she could grab them out of his chubby pink hands and replace them.

It made me smile.

Funerals just weren't the same without children around. It made me realize right then and there that life does not stop— not for broken hearts, not for the Mexicans next door, not for burnt out morticians, not even for tall, smoking men. Life does not wait for you to catch up or even lick your wounds. Only the dead people had peace.

I thought of Jake, grunting and straining to drop that huge rock into the lake, and I smiled inwardly at the thought of that strange freckled boy who knew more about being alive than anyone else I had ever known.

The world seemed right again.

When I arrived back at the mortuary, Lisa was waiting for me with a small glass vase filled with white roses. "Louise..." she purred, passing them in front of me playfully, "guess who these are for..."

I frowned at her and snatched the small card from the bouquet. She followed me into the lounge, her little heels clacking behind me. I opened the card. It said:

I adore you,
Jake.

"Who are they from?" Lisa asked, trying to peek over my shoulder.

I blushed and held the card to my breast.

"Just some guy I have been seeing." I showed her the card and we fawned over it together.

Lisa jumped up and down and made little sounds. "Oh, I am so happy for you. I wish that Robert would send me a card like that."

We chatted and I told her some of Jake's finer points.

"You know, it's funny." Lisa mused aloud, looking at me carefully, "but I always kind of thought that you and Martin would get together."

I looked at Jake's card and thought about how precious and boy-like his messy handwriting was scrawled on it. His letters were thin, long, and went up on the ends. "Martin and me?" I said, laughing to her but quiet inside, "We would beat each other senseless in a week."

She laughed. "Oh gosh, I guess that would be true, wouldn't it?"

"Besides that," I added for good measure, "I hate him."

"Hate who?" Martin's voice rang as he entered the room. He didn't wait for an answer when he saw the white roses on the table. "Who are those for?"

Lisa tried to snatch the card from my hand but I had too good a grip on it. She told Martin, "They are for Lou, from a male admirer."

I noted Martin's tiny change like a tic in his facial expression from curious to that of resignation. He nodded his head slightly toward me. I looked away quickly, stuffing the card into the pocket of my charcoal grey suit jacket.

Lisa was arranging the flowers with her tiny hands, "Aren't they beautiful? I would give anything to get flowers at work." She sighed dreamily. "And white, you know that white is such a pure color. Most guys would have just sent red, but this is better. This is true and pure."

I smiled in spite of myself. It was true and pure.

Martin poured himself a cup of coffee and patted the chest pocket that contained his cigarette pack and lighter unconsciously, his way of reassuring himself that the world was still in order.

He adores me, I thought, exiting the lounge and sashaying dreamily through the long corridor past the boxes of crucifixes, candles, plastic urns stacked high upon one another, and empty caskets still wrapped in plastic from the manufacturer waiting on rolling carts for their eternal occupants.

I looked at myself in the hallway mirror— my Mexican nose and my dark eyes and my lips that always seemed too small for my face. I smiled at myself like a buffoon. *He adores me.*

I entered the back office area and saw Hank snoring with his head on his desk, his arms hanging down so that the backs of his huge fingers touched the short carpet. Papers from his latest case were strewn about the desk in front of him and underneath his head. He was drooling onto his obituary form. He looked dead.

Troy came bouncing through; on a search for a lost file (he was always misplacing his things). Troy saw Hank sleeping and made a face like he was puking when he saw Hank's drool. Troy's fake puking caused me to try to hold back a laugh, which came out as more of a snort, which in turn woke Hank up, who rubbed his eyes groggily and stared at us like we were crazy as he wiped the drool from his chin— the drool of the almost-dead.

Life's finer moments wouldn't be nearly so precious if it lasted forever.

(The dead people taught me this.)

CHAPTER 32

I kept on seeing Jake, only now I would invite him in after our dates. I took great liberties with him after that initial kiss.

I remembered our first overnight trip together. I was so nervous and he was so charming. He borrowed his parents' car so I could have air conditioning. He planned our route carefully in the map book and played drumbeats on my legs with his hands as we drove along.

In the morning he still smelled like warm buttered toast, and I laughed when he woke up with his shoulder-length hair loose from its neat ponytail and in serious disarray. I thought about how I was the only one who got to see him like that, with no glasses and his hair all asunder.

I asked him why he came back all those times after I would send him home with just a handshake. He said, "I was waiting for you to realize that you were going to be my wife."

Jake was a bolt of electricity in a world full of dead people.

I would love to twist it into some sort of heart-wrenching, passionate affair— but in truth my relationship with Jake was filled with laughter and light, and was so different from what I thought love was supposed to be, that I had almost let it slip right past me. Depression and darkness were not an identity; they were not my identity... not anymore.

Narcissism and search for deeper meaning bred together on a bed of confusion and loneliness. Maybe this was what Aaron had been trying to teach me all along. Aaron had constantly chastised me about feeling too proud when I had cosmetized or embalmed a great case. *"Give it to God,"* He told me over and over. He was trying to save me from falling into the trap where being a great mortician was my only treasure. He was trying to take the pain of ego away from me. I did not understand it until later on. Aaron was trying to save me from his fate, or perhaps from the fate of Joel, whose entire worth was invested within a perfect piece of sculpted wax. Or maybe even from Hank's fate, who remained locked in perpetual agony, unable to admit that he no longer wanted to come to the mortuary and sit with crying families, or that he would sooner sit in the bathroom all day than wait for the next death call to come in. Or maybe still, Aaron was trying to warn of the elusive owner's fate; in which the desire to perform in funeral service had left so completely that he could no longer bear to even step foot on the property.

Or perhaps the owner was having the biggest laugh of all, collecting his paycheck and playing golf while his staff did the dirty work. Perhaps.

"Some people are bred for funeral service," Aaron told me one day, nodding towards Troy, who was closing a service in our chapel with grand flourish. "Troy will probably never burn out, because to him, it is a presentation, a show. He has funeral service in a safe place."

I nodded, thinking how Troy was indeed unaffected by the rigors of funeral service.

"Some, like Martin, possess a natural grace and elegance," Aaron continued.

I turned towards Aaron slightly, still keeping my hands in front of me in funeral director position. I decided to confront him with something that had been eating at my insecurities for some time, "And what do I have? Why are choosing me to replace you instead of someone like Martin or Troy?"

"Because you have heart," he answered. "Because if I lost someone, I would want you to help me."

I never got to answer because people started getting up from their pews and it was our job to dismiss them in an orderly fashion past the casket and out the side door to await the procession to the cemetery.

Aaron never threw a lot of compliments my way— and so I remembered every one.

CHAPTER 33

We received the body of a twenty-year old woman that was embalmed and transported in from Mexico by way of a low-riding beat-up black station wagon. The back window had been knocked out so that the back hatch would close. The wagon popped up a couple of relieved inches when we slid the casket out of its back end. I could hear the car's suspension sigh in relief to be rid of the heavy burden. The Mexican driver, clad in jeans, dusty boots, and a t-shirt waved to us and tore back out of our back lot, blasting mariachi music out the missing back window.

We led the casket into our preparation room for a customary final inspection before taking it into our chapel for viewing.

Caskets from Mexico appeared thinner and less sturdy than those made in the United States. They often had a clear glass plate which prevented the body from being touched. We always thought this was because the quality of Mexico's embalming was poor and bodies tended to need a lot of restoration and heavy cosmetics that they did not want people to be able to touch and smear off during the viewing. This casket was constructed of uneven wood planks covered with an embossed dark blue fabric. The smell of chemicals and decomposition coming from inside the casket caused us to wrinkle our noses at one another even before we opened the casket to look inside.

"Oh, I don't think I even want to look," I said, closing the preparation room doors behind us.

Martin raised the casket lid and grimaced, and together we surveyed the damage.

One eyelid was shrunken hard as leather and black, the other eyelid was puffy, green, and moist, the outer layers of skin beginning to slough off revealing dark red underneath, the tell-tale signs of decomposition. The Mexican officials had performed a post-mortem exam, or an autopsy, upon her body and the embalmer had sealed the incisions on her head and chest improperly, causing leakage of body and embalming fluids from multiple gapes in the sutures.

Pale fluids from her cranial cavity stained the cream-colored pillow beneath her head. Dark pink fluids from her thoracic and abdominal cavities wicked out into her white satin dress that now that I inspected more closely, appeared to be a wedding dress. The Embalmer had hiked the dress high up to her chin to cover the straight autopsy incision that they used in Mexico. Instead of a 'Y' incision like we used in the States, doctors there made a single cut from pubis to throat. I pulled the dress back from her neck and saw that it indeed was a wedding dress with a low v-neckline. The neckline had been pulled and bunched up high to cover the hideously sutured autopsy incision. The delicate lace around the edge of the neckline was stained with pink and brown tinged fluids, wrinkled, and stiff.

As Martin and I stared at the young woman's body together in silence, a fat white maggot wriggled its way out of the corner of her puffy eyelid and rolled onto the stained pillow, turning blindly about in protest to the new light.

Martin and I looked at each other. The viewing was tonight, in our chapel. In four hours. *Four hours!*

Now we were faced with a quandary here— first of all, this was not our case, we were merely renting out our chapel to the Mexican funeral home so that the family could have their viewing. The other funeral home would return tomorrow to collect the casket and deliver it to the local cemetery. Technically, we were only renting out a chapel and attendants for an evening viewing... technically, we were not involved beyond this. We did not prepare the woman's body. We were not being compensated to do preparation work on the woman's body. However, if we put a body out for viewing in this condition in our chapel guests would only know to blame us. The people would never know and never care who prepared the body. The people would never understand that it wasn't our fault. Even though we were merely just apprentice embalmers, we were trained and conditioned to buffer families from the harsh reality of decomposition and putrefaction, to preserve dignity and cleanliness, and to present a peaceful and meaningful last memory... some may argue that it may not have been the most noble mission on earth— but it was our mission.

There was nothing for us to do but try and fix her ourselves.

Martin and I looked at each other with fire in our eyes and began work immediately. With only four hours left until her viewing, there was no time to waste. We never had to discuss the significance of things. We always moved in perfect unison at work.

No wonder the guy who dropped her off had sped out of there like a bat out of hell, I thought, as I tied my lab coat around my waist. I wouldn't have wanted to stay and account for a mess like that, either.

We slid straps around the woman and lifted her body from the smelly casket. By now Lisa was in the preparation room with her phone headset still clipped to her collar and the unattached cord dangling loose, voicing her disgust over the condition of the body and talking trash about Mexican embalmers.

The dead lady had been a pretty woman once— we could see that as we lowered her body by straps onto an embalming table. Her long, thick brown hair was tangled and knotted up within the sloppy stitches of her head incision, crusted with dried fluid in some parts and still oozing from others.

Once we had her on the table, we stepped back for a moment. We looked at the mess before us— the stained and crusty dress, the leaky incisions, the rotten casket. It seemed like an impossible task. We now had three hours and forty-two minutes.

We removed the dress and handed it off to Lisa, who was waiting with gloves over her manicured nails and a bottle of carpet stain lifter. Her heels click-clacked quickly over to the sink and water began running.

Martin grabbed an aneurysm hook and scissors and began to pull and cut through the string that held the chest incision together. I did likewise on the head incision, trying simultaneously to detangle her hair and remove some of the crusty chunks from it. We used cotton and phenol to cauterize and dry out the moist tissues inside the cavities and to help mask the overwhelming and unmistakable smell of rotting human remains. Martin re-bagged her viscera and surrounded it with a clean smelling and preserving powdered chemical, replaced her breastplate, dusted some sealing powder throughout and began suturing her chest and abdomen with an airtight baseball stitch. I packed the cranium and used metal head-clamps to re-attach the top of the calvarium back onto her skull. I was careful as I sutured her scalp to make sure her long hair did not bunch up and get caught in the thread. I tried to be patient with the tedious process as the clock on the preparation room wall hungrily ate the minutes. How many times had I been in that room, racing that old grey clock? Too many to count.

I grabbed the hose and began to wash her hair with germicidal soap, lathering it up again and again, working through to the tangled ends with my gloved fingers, and then rinsing endless chunks of congealed powders, fluids, and filth down the table.

When Martin reached the top part of the incision on the woman's chest, the part that would show when the dress was fitted properly and not bunched up around her chin, he switched to an intricate hidden stitch. This stitch would draw the ends on the skin under, leaving a smooth, slightly inward beveled line without visible threads, making it possible for us the fill the line above the neckline of her dress with wax and cosmetize it until it was no longer noticeable.

Next we washed her entire body down with germicidal soap and disinfectant spray, guiding tangled lumps of hair, soggy pieces of skin slip, maggots, and clumps of sealing powder down the drain and into the disposal.

I dried her off with white hand towels while Martin busied himself with the task of pressing the wax between his hands to make it warm and pliable. Normally, waxing and cosmetizing was something we would do after dressing was completed, but Lisa was still scrubbing out the wet dress over the sink and there was no time to spare.

I sprayed detangler on her long hair and brushed and dried until it was smooth. I looked at the clock as my hands worked automatically, adrenaline washing through my stomach.

Next Martin and I studied her face together. Her eyelashes had sloughed off along with their surrounding decomposed tissues. Her eyelids would need to be rebuilt with wax, and in order for us to accomplish this, we needed to dry them out and make them hard. Wax only worked if we had a good, solid, dry surface for it to adhere to. We would have to use an electric spatula to reduce and cauterize these delicate tissues by way of heat. The spatula was actually a few inch long, flattened tube of metal with a smooth plastic handle and a long cord that when plugged into a socket, would heat the metal part to a high temperature.

As apprentices, we were in over our heads on this one. We had not had enough experience in major restorations and I wished that Aaron had not gone with Troy on an out-of-town service that day. I wished he could have been there to guide us. I had only read about the electric spatula in my embalming textbook, but Martin said he had seen Joel use it once so I plugged it in and handed it to him.

He applied a layer of white tissue cream over the first eyelid like he told me he watched Joel do and made his first unsure pass over the tissue, causing the tissue cream to hiss and pop and run down the woman's cheeks in melted brown rivulets. A couple more passes, a little more tissue cream and we smiled at each other. *It worked.* The skin on her eyelid was markedly reduced in bloating and became firmer with each pass of the hot instrument.

Lisa had gotten most of the stains out of the dress and was trying diligently to dry it out by running a hot iron over it.

About that time Hank sauntered in on his way to the employee bathroom at the end of the preparation room. He stopped and raised one eyebrow when he saw the wreckage spread out— the naked woman on the embalming table with the green abdomen, the open casket made by some foreign manufacturer with the soiled pillow in it, Martin standing with the hissing spatula in his hand and sweat running down his brow, me digging through the cabinets looking for something that we could kill maggots with.

After he took a silent inventory, Hank narrowed his eyes, ready to pull rank on Martin and me. "What are you doing?" he asked.

"I'm cleaning a dress," Lisa said good-naturedly, saluting Hank with her iron.

Hank did not respond to her, but continued bouncing his glare between me and Martin. I had the feeling that Hank expected us to explain ourselves to him; after all, he did consider it 'his' preparation room. There was tension in the air and I realized that he was not going to leave until either Martin or I answered him.

"We're racing the clock," Martin finally told him quickly, continuing to press and sear the woman's eyelids back into compliance.

"This body was already prepared. This was not our case," Hank stated gruffly, resting his large ruddy hands on his ample hips.

No one answered him. Lisa sensed the change in the atmosphere in the room and lowered her head to resume ironing.

"Nobody paid us to get her body ready. They are just renting our chapel," Hank said. He walked over and looked at the body closely, watching as Martin plucked a small wriggling maggot from the woman's nostril and dropped it down into the disposal. "This was not our case," Hank repeated, louder this time.

Still nobody answered.

I pulled something called 'Maggot-No-More' down from the chemical shelves and studied it carefully so I didn't have to look at Hank. But deep inside, my ire began to rise, and I wondered if Martin wasn't feeling the same. Martin and I weren't tenderfoots anymore, my inside voice raged. Martin and I were the ones who covered for Hank every time in the past two years when he needed to sit in the bathroom all day, and every time he called in sick. Martin and I were the ones who took the calls in the afternoons when Hank took a death certificate to the next town for a doctor's signature and didn't come back until his shift was over.

As far as I was concerned, Hank had abdicated the throne. He had no right to question us anymore. It was our preparation room now. I put the bottle of Maggot-No-More down, turned, and stared at Hank in silence, making it a point to not lower my gaze before he did.

"She is viewing in our chapel," I finally said, more aggressively than I meant to sound, "She is our case now."

I saw Martin look up at the wall clock and then continue working on the eyelids.

"I still don't think it is our responsibility to fix someone else's mistake." Hank took a step back and began to look at the casket. He clucked his tongue when he saw the stained pillow and interior. "This is exactly how people take advantage of us. They don't want to pay our prices for good work and they know that we will fix whatever crap people bring in for free. This is how it has always been. People always looking to save a buck... hustling it out from under the real embalmers." He huffed and puffed about as he lectured us.

I read the instructions on the back of the Maggot-No-More bottle. It looked old. The label was peeling off and the metal cap had begun to corrode. There was about a half an inch of congealed amber colored fluid settled at the bottom.

"I'll tell you one thing, if I was in charge, this wouldn't be happening right now," Hank spat.

I bit down on my tongue to stop myself from saying something to him that would take us to an ugly place. I might be him one day, I told myself, chewing on Aaron's sharp warnings like I was chewing on glass. I imagined blood spilling out of my mouth and down the front of my white lab coat.

I noticed that Martin's neck was growing red and a small blue vein began to pulse near his temple. I knew we were moments away from an explosion of anger. I briefly wondered what would happen if the two men, both over six foot and strong, were to come to blows. I had seen this coming before, the two men sometimes stomping around each other like bulls in a pen, but Martin always backed down like a gentleman, humbling himself before the more experienced (and licensed) Hank. The times when Hank was obviously abusing his authority or just being plain lazy, Martin would patiently acquiesce to his outrageous demands— the plight of the apprentice. Hank was harder on Martin than he was on me, because Martin was a male, therefore, Martin was inherently more of a threat to his ego. But Martin was done with his apprenticeship now, he was going to school next semester, and the invisible force of power ebbing and flowing was all around us.

As inexplicable as it was sudden, Hank abruptly turned and walked out of the preparation room. He glanced back at me and motioned to the bottle in my hand, "You'll never get rid of the maggots with that crap!" He slammed the door closed behind him; leaving

Martin, Lisa, and I to shake our heads at one another in exasperation.

"What an asshole," Martin said.

"I guess he was too busy to actually help us out or anything," Lisa said sarcastically. "He didn't use to be like this."

I was trying to control my anger, but I had already decided if I saw Hank again that day that I would tell him what a louse I thought he was. I didn't care what Aaron would say. I vowed that I would never end up like Hank.

I looked skeptically at the bottle in my hand. Hank was probably right about the Maggot-No-More being no good— a fact that just angered me more. I went over to Martin to help with inserting the woman's new eyelashes that we had made by cutting off small pieces of her hair and inserting them two or three at a time into the wax. It was a tedious and delicate process. I kept thinking that all of this fancy work was going to be of small consolation to the grieving family when maggots came popping out of her nostrils. Maggots, the plague of the Embalmer, with their waxy outer coating that made them impervious to our harshest chemicals. I knew by listening to people talk at Mortuary College that most of the products that were supposed to kill maggots in dead bodies only had so-so results. Nature was unstoppable.

Committed still, but now with a little less confidence, we continued our work. Joel taught me this procedure, and as I applied the hairs I had memories of Joel's wax head. I wondered if God's plan for Joel's life involved meeting me to show me how to fix the Mexican girl's face. Would God go through the trouble of stringing together such a domino chain of eventuality?

Suddenly the preparation room door burst open and Hank came marching in carrying a little jar of fluid in his hand. Before any of us had a chance to speak, Hank threw the jar underhand in my direction. By reflex I reached hastily to catch it so it would not fall and break. "Its kerosene," Hank said, turning back towards the door. I turned the bottle over in my hands, inspecting the caramel colored fluid. "Put it up her nose and it should hold the maggots until the viewing is over." The preparation room door slammed behind him once more and he was gone.

"Well, I'll be a monkey's uncle," Martin said.

I was not sure why, but I laughed a strange laugh, causing Martin and Lisa to look at me as if I had just passed gas.

"I don't care what anyone says... he is still a jerk," Martin said, throwing me a look. "I mean, he threw the bottle at you, if it had fallen and broke, we would still be screwed."

"But it didn't break," Lisa reminded him.

"But it could have!" Martin said in an irritated tone. "One day that boy and me are going to have to settle this around the back of the barn."

"Hank would kick your ass," I told Martin tauntingly, suddenly aware I had no more anger for the brooding and fragile Hank. "He outweighs you by about 75 pounds!"

Martin straightened himself up and puffed up like a rooster, "That's just it, baby, I am leaner and faster! I would have his fat-ass on the ground before he knew what hit him." He jutted out his chin and demonstrated some karate hand chops in the air.

"Okay there, fists-of-fury," I said, causing Lisa to snicker. I handed him the jar of kerosene. "Start packing her nose."

The minutes became hours. We scrambled about. We pried her still damp (but clean) dress back on her and Martin and I lifted her by hand back into the casket. Lisa had found a new casket pillow that was almost the same shade as the casket lining and we tossed the old stained pillow. Martin and I dabbed makeup gently over the wax, dappling in shades of tans, reds, and browns and blended, blended, blended the way Joel had instructed me until the pink wax on her face and chest was covered and the continuity of undamaged skin reappeared in its place. I could smell the scent of kerosene wafting up from her nostrils. We ran Q-tips dipped in Dry Wash painstakingly across her new eyelashes and eyebrows to remove the heavy facial makeup from their strands. Lisa, who by now was completely invested in our mission, wrapped tendrils of long dark hair around a hot curling iron and hummed to herself as she arranged the hair beautifully about the dead woman's face and shoulders.

"Ten minutes to view!" Martin cried suddenly, picking last pieces of stray hair and cotton from the woman's dress and casket.

I closed the bottom half of the casket and locked it into place. Lisa grabbed her combs and hair spray off the casket edge so that Martin could replace the glass on top of the casket.

"Can you smell kerosene?" I asked, sniffing around after the glass lid was locked into place.

"The flowers should cover it up." Martin answered.

We heard the front bell sound that meant someone came in the front door and all three of us simultaneously peered up at the security monitor. We saw a large group of dark haired people in fancy clothes in the lobby, waiting to be shown into the chapel. The woman's family was here.

"I'll go stall them for a few minutes... but you guys'd better hurry," Lisa said, peeling off her exam gloves quickly and clacking off down the hallway.

Martin and I raced the casket through the familiar back hallway stretch and into the back of the chapel. We raced the casket into position so fast that Aaron would have fainted from worry if he'd been present, and parked it under the red and yellow makeup lights. Then we hastily moved some of the floral arrangements into place around the wooden bier that the casket rested on.

"She looks awfully made up," I said, pausing to look at the woman.

"Well... that's because she is."

"Maybe we should use one of those sheer drapes in the closet."

"That is an excellent idea and I am glad that I thought of it," Martin said with a smirk.

We draped a sheer blue chiffon casket drape over the top end of the casket and I breathed out. That was it, I knew. We had finished, and we had finished on time. Relief washed through me.

The tiny holes in the material acted as a refining lens, and softened the opaque cosmetics. She remained perfectly visible, but her imperfections faded beneath the hazy barrier. She looked quite beautiful. I stood there in that moment thinking that maybe there is value sometimes in not being able to see so clearly. Maybe that was why Martin and my Mom blew smoke around themselves every day. Maybe they were trying to make things appear softer, less harsh.

"Wow." Martin said, taking one last long look at the Mexican woman in her casket.

While he stood there, I stared at his strong profile and smiled as he fussed over the chiffon drape one last time. It wasn't going to get any more perfect, but in the fussing was how funeral directors showed that they cared. Joel used to fuss for hours, picking at invisible pieces of hair and lint, straightening already perfect ties again and again, right up until the family walked in sometimes— this was an unspoken sign of dedication and personal investment.

I watched Martin's lined face, bent seriously over the casket as he set about straightening the chiffon with the importance and earnestness of a doctor performing surgery.

Dear Martin, I thought, how could anyone not see the beauty in your tall grace—
your stiff elegance—
and your overwhelming
(and ever mounting)
fear?

CHAPTER 34

Martin and I walked slowly and tiredly out past the hearse and towards the employee parking area. It was dark. I began to feel the excitement in my belly that I always felt when I knew that I was about to see Jake.

I let out my breath and ran my hands through my disheveled hair.

"Are we eating?" Martin asked.

"Definitely," I told him, stretching out the kinks in my neck.

After a short pause, he said, "Do you think Jake would want to come?"

I smiled, "I think he would."

"I'm kind of feeling like pancakes."

We walked out into the cool night, Martin and me, who bridged our differences by a mutual respect for the art of embalming and body restoration. It was the only thing we had ever really agreed upon, anyhow. The love and the passion to do the work that God had given us the gift to perform.

I breathed in the free air.

Martin produced his cigarettes and lighter from his chest pocket. The deep hollows of his face flashed for an instance in the darkness when he lit up. His steel blue eyes met mine as smoke filled up the space between us.

EPILOGUE

One year later, Martin left to start Mortuary College. Aaron left to pursue his higher education (but not before he fired Hank for calling in sick for a whole week so that he could embalm at night for a rival mortuary). Lisa accepted a job offer as secretary at the local cemetery. Very suddenly, Troy and I were the senior people, left to guide the mortuary through its next phase of life and death.

I finally got to meet the owner. He was a short, round little man with nervous ticks and he smiled a lot and didn't look you in the eye for more than a few seconds at a time. His hands were always fidgeting and I learned quickly that he preferred to discuss what movies were coming out over the state of the budget. I was given his personal phone number and informed to call him whenever needed, followed by "…but only if it's really important…"

Troy and I folded new employees into the fray as each old one went away.

Truth be told, I didn't feel like I was ready for the huge responsibility of training new Funeral Directors and Embalmers, but Aaron assured me that the person in charge never feels ready. "You start looking around wondering where all the mentors went," Aaron told me, "and then you realize that everyone else is looking at you. That is how it works."

We inducted Lyn, the bright and cheery new secretary who decorated her desk with angels and fresh flowers and made sure our collars were straight before we went on services. Next we welcomed Lori, a beautiful, petite young apprentice embalmer from Kansas, who was as strong as an ox and had a mouth like a sailor. Last but not least came Quang, a licensed Embalmer with a heavy Vietnamese accent and in a hurry to do all things, until Troy took him under his wing and helped him slow things down a bit.

I would hear Troy counseling Quang on occasion over our new cubicles.

"Dude… when you answer the phone, slow down, I can't even tell what you are saying," Troy would say.

"I twy answa phone so I may hep them," Quang would tell him quickly and passionately.

"I know, but when you rush it sounds like, 'herro,-this-is-fish-hum-mutua-way-can-I-hep-you?' Dude! I'll bet the people are like… WHERE in the hell did I just call?! Fish-hummer mutty?!"

"I no sound rike dat!" Quang would say, getting frustrated. "I try heping customah."

"And another thing… don't be so quick to answer the phone, next time, either. Let it ring a couple times… you don't want people to think we are sitting around like

vultures waiting to pounce on a new death..." Troy
lectured.

"I no pounce rike vurture! You pounce rike vurture!
I heping customah!"

Somehow Troy would work his magic and get Quang
laughing about the whole business of being a mortician
and then they would go out for lunch at the deli across
the street like regular chums.

I never forgot about the old staff. As my career grew
I went through many different phases of employees, I
saw the old familiar demon of burnout always waiting
and watching for its next victim. If you built a wall, it
climbed higher. If you ran, it was there waiting when
you fell. I watched the bright young faces come in full
of optimism and bravado, and I remembered the day I
walked in wearing my best white sweater (the fluffy kind
that made you want to reach out and touch it), full of the
best intentions and ready to change the world.

I wanted to protect my staff from this fate, but the
task was tremendous, and in the end, each person had to
decide if funeral directing was really what they wanted to
spend their lives doing. Funeral directors like Troy were
a rare lot.

Jake and I got married and moved Harold the cat and
I out of the apartment with the elevator that smelled of
urine and into a fancy condominium on the other side of
town. I cherished every freckle on Jake's body. I began
to think that maybe Aaron's God wasn't so angry after
all. How could an angry God let something like love
exist? Caught up in the enigma of my condition and the
fear that I had no one to communicate even a sliver of
my essence to— I had almost failed to recognize love. I

thought of all those times I had shut the door in Jake's face instead of inviting him inside; shaking his hand brusquely instead of offering a hug or a kiss... was it God's plan that gave Jake the fortitude to keep coming back? How did Jake know that he only had to wait a little longer for me to come around? Harold slept on Jake's side of the bed now, nestled into the hair of his undone ponytail.

I am alive.

I never forgot about the stabbed girl or the howling mother or the old man at the cemetery who grabbed my arms so hard... I never forgot any of the dead people— they just weren't all I thought about anymore. I think that is all right. Funeral Directors dealt in flesh, and flesh is messy. Most people walked around never conceiving of what lie a couple of centimeters deep— beneath the layers of integument... the twisting intestines, the moving fluids, the collecting tumors— the brute mechanics that operated beneath our feeble quest for virtue, love, and beauty.

I am alive.

There was no sense to be made out of any of it, except to say that I was changed by the things I had seen; that is, after all, the human condition. I outgrew my childish dreams of trying to change the world.

In the end, I kept Aaron's words of wisdom above all others—

practice the art of embalming—

and give the rest to God.

I am alive.

Acknowledgments

Thanks to Miki-Mama, my lifelong supporter and inspirational muse. I am indebted to Lyn Talone, my dear friend and the best editor ever (thanks for always telling me the way it is, Babes). Many thanks to Dave McCament, my mentor and friend. Hot, juicy thanks to Jeffrey, who reminded me that I am still alive. And special thanks to my little Rembrandt Lenore— the precious baby girl who forced me to be a better person.

This book is dedicated to the nameless, faceless (and under-thanked) ranks of Funeral Directors and Embalmers who man the front-lines of death day after day while the rest of the world slumbers peacefully.

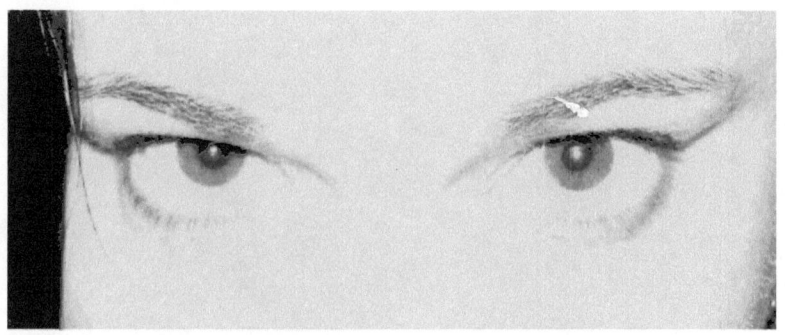

Amber Lenore Winckler is a 1995 graduate of Cypress College of Mortuary Science. She is a California licensed Funeral Director, Embalmer, and Crematory Manager. Amber formerly was the General Manager of Alhiser-Comer Mortuary and Lakepointe Crematory located in Escondido, California. She also worked as a Forensic Autopsy Assistant at the San Diego Medical Examiner's Office— she was the first woman ever hired for this position in the history of San Diego County. She currently writes full-time and is an active Trade Embalmer.

Website:
amberwinckler.com